A quick tu̶r̶ W9-DHT-079 drapery ended and Anna was back on the catwalk.

Even though the blaring music made it impossible to hear anything else, the incessant click of cameras echoed as flashes went off around her.

Then it happened. The heel of the right shoe snapped. Thrown off balance, she stumbled once, twice, then pitched to the side and off the catwalk. In that moment, she heard the collective gasp of the crowd, the frantic clicking of the cameras, her own heartbeat thundering as the wisps of her skirt flew up into her face and thankfully shrouded her in her most humiliating moment.

She landed in someone's lap. She couldn't see who, but she could feel him. *Most definitely a him*, she thought as strong arms wrapped around her and steadied her. Her body registered the muscular chest she was clasped against, the spicy amber scent rolling off her rescuer that simultaneously teased her with its familiarity and comforted her.

"I'm so sorry, I..."

Her words trailed off as she pushed the material down and met the glittering brown eyes of the man she'd once loved.

Antonio Cabrera.

The Infamous Cabrera Brothers

They're undeniably tempting...and unexpectedly tempted!

One's brooding, one's scandalous, one's mysterious...

Everyone knows who the Cabrera brothers are. Their billion-dollar business ventures have put them on the map, and their devilishly handsome looks turn heads the world over.

But truly getting to know the tall, dark and Spanish bachelors? That's something only three exceptional women will have the pleasure of...

Read Adrian's story in
His Billion-Dollar Takeover Temptation

Read Alejandro's story in
Proof of Their One Hot Night

And discover Antonio's story in
A Deal for the Tycoon's Diamonds

All available now!

Emmy Grayson

A DEAL FOR THE TYCOON'S DIAMONDS

HARLEQUIN
PRESENTS

Recycling programs for this product may not exist in your area.

ISBN-13: 978-1-335-56945-5

A Deal for the Tycoon's Diamonds

Copyright © 2022 by Emmy Grayson

This edition published by arrangement with Harlequin Books S.A.

For questions and comments about the quality of this book, please contact us at CustomerService@Harlequin.com.

Harlequin Enterprises ULC
22 Adelaide St. West, 41st Floor
Toronto, Ontario M5H 4E3, Canada
www.Harlequin.com

Printed in U.S.A.

Emmy Grayson wrote her first book at the age of seven about a spooky ghost. Her passion for romance novels began a few years later with the discovery of a worn copy of Kathleen E. Woodiwiss's *A Rose in Winter* buried on her mother's bookshelf. She lives in the Midwest countryside with her husband (who's also her ex-husband), their baby boy and enough animals to start their own zoo.

Books by Emmy Grayson

Harlequin Presents

The Infamous Cabrera Brothers

His Billion-Dollar Takeover Temptation
Proof of Their One Hot Night

Visit the Author Profile page
at Harlequin.com for more titles.

To the people who provided me with love, support and the most epic lakeside game of Cards Against Humanity this summer, thank you.

CHAPTER ONE

Rome, Italy

LIGHTS FLASHED AS techno music pulsed through Anna Vega's veins. She stopped on the catwalk, bestowed a shaky Mona Lisa smile to the nearest camera and then cursed inwardly. Hadn't someone told her *not* to smile, to look mysterious and aloof?

Too late now. Besides, she needed to concentrate on walking. One foot in front of the other on sky-high heels that were a feat of engineering. The shoes, a silver creation covered in sapphires, clicked on the glass walkway. The crystal-clear waters of the courtyard fountain bubbled behind her as she stopped for one last look before she disappeared behind the drapes and headed toward the room off the hotel courtyard that housed the rest of the models and their entourages.

Before she could suck in a breath, she walked through the double glass doors and into the waiting arms of half a dozen stylists.

"Brush out Anna's hair!"

"No, no, the petal for her lips, not vixen!"

"Final dress is the tulle and organza!"

Anna closed her eyes, not letting the crowd pulsing around her witness her conflicting feelings of pride and pain. The final dress she would wear tonight, a gown with a full skirt and a deep neckline, was in honor of her mother. The skirt, a nod to the first formal dress her mother had bought her for family Christmas photos when she was four years old. The top, a nod to the countless times her mother had mentioned that one day she would get the confidence to wear something "just a little more daring." A day that had never come thanks to a reckless driver on a Louisiana bayou backroad.

Yet her mother would be proud, too. The first design she'd created that was truly her own. No replicating, no playing it safe. No, this one was *hers*.

Although, Anna contended as she opened her eyes, she wouldn't have made the plunge neckline quite so deep if she'd known she would be the one to wear it. But when Kess had called her up and told her that she needed Anna and would she please fly to Rome immediately with a suitcase of her designs, she'd put the dress and a few of her old passable works into a case and gone.

Except now she'd been catapulted from slow to light speed. What had started off as filling in some holes in Kess's first fashion show after a designer had pulled out had turned into her debut as a model when one of the girls had come down with food poisoning.

In classic Kess style, aside from a slight tightening of her lips, she hadn't shown how much each blow had stressed her out. No, she'd just sighed and plowed forward, determined to make her first show a success. When she'd approached Anna with the modeling request, it had terrified her. But Kess had always been there for her. It had been time for Anna to step up.

The gold of her dress shimmered beneath the lights backstage. A departure from the pastels she normally favored. She used to love the airiness, the crisp feeling, when she slid on something white. But after that damned article, all she saw was bland. Boring.

Virginal.

Even now she cringed at the picture of her that had been selected, the sensationalized text beneath. Although, she acknowledged with a slight smile, that article had at least done some good. In a moment of blazing *I'll show them* anger, she'd ordered the fabric that had turned into this dress.

"You okay?"

Anna opened her eyes to see Kess standing in front of her. Violet silk clung to the newest producer of Hampton Events's statuesque frame, stopping just short of her ankles. A seductive drape gave the audience a glimpse of the sparkles a makeup artist had dusted across Kess's ebony chest. She looked stunning.

Anna tried to give her friend a confident smile as someone tugged the fluffy layers of the skirt down over her legs. "A little different than T-shirts and sweatpants for late-night studying?"

Kess smiled as the concern disappeared. "A little. We're definitely not in Granada anymore."

"Kess!"

The stage manager's bellow cut through the cacophony of voices, hair dryers and music blaring over the crowd. Kess squeezed Anna's hand and hurried away. Two seconds later, the manager yelled for Anna to get in place.

She tapped the toe of her matching gold heel on the ground as butterflies danced in her chest.

One last walk. One last walk and then you're done and you never have to do this again.

Getting outside of her comfort zone was one thing. Being the center of attention was something else entirely.

"Last walk," she muttered to herself. "You can do it, you can do it."

The assistant in charge of the curtain glanced at her and then looked away, a small smile on his face. Compared to the legions of models he'd most likely seen over his career, she probably seemed ridiculous. Inexperienced.

Imposter syndrome reared its vicious head.

What was she doing here? She wasn't a model. She was a barely there fashion designer who had only recently gotten noticed because of a magazine article that had focused more on her personal choices than her art. Even then, the interest had been fleeting, the majority of the requests related to her very loose relationship with one of the wealthiest families in Europe. The couple of inquiries on her actual work hadn't gone past portfolio requests.

She bit down on her lower lip. A nervous habit she'd developed as a child, one she'd mostly overcome. But moments like these brought it back; when she felt out of her depth and was thrust into the body of a frightened little girl who'd just lost her parents and heard over and over again that she would be protected, shielded from the cruelties of the world. Who, every time she had tried to venture out on her own, was faced with more restrictions, more rules, more questions about whether she was capable of doing this or that on her own. Over time, hearing how much her aunt and uncle didn't think she was strong had sunk into her bones. Her parents' deaths had changed her, zapped so much of who'd she been and left her hollowed out by grief, that she'd accepted their overbearing coddling, allowed herself to eventually believe that she was weak and needed others to depend on.

Except for one. She shook her head. No, he'd

always encouraged her, told her she could do anything, be anyone.

Just not his lover.

She scrunched her eyes shut against the memory. Now was not the time to be thinking of one of her biggest failures.

"Go!"

The assistant's voice banished the last bits of the past. She opened her eyes, squared her shoulders and walked forward. A quick turn to the right after the drapery ended and she was back on the catwalk. Even though the blaring music made it impossible to hear almost anything else, the incessant click of cameras echoed as flashes went off around her.

Then it happened. The heel of the right shoe snapped. Thrown off balance, she stumbled once, twice, then pitched to the side and off the catwalk. In that moment, she heard the collective gasp of the crowd, the frantic clicking of the cameras, her own heartbeat thundering as the wisps of her skirt flew up into her face and thankfully blinded her to her most humiliating moment.

She landed in someone's lap. She couldn't see who, but she could feel him. *Most definitely a him*, she thought as strong arms wrapped around her and steadied her. Despite the severity of the moment, her body registered the muscular chest she was clasped against, the spicy amber scent rolling off her rescuer that simultaneously teased her with its familiarity and comforted her.

"I'm so sorry, I…" Her words trailed off as she pushed the material down and met the glittering brown eyes of the man she'd once loved.

Antonio Cabrera.

The world returned in a rush as the flashes intensified. Her first instinct was to hide her face in her hands, to try to slink off into the crowd and hope the paparazzi wouldn't follow.

Coward.

She swallowed hard. No matter how tempting, running away wouldn't solve anything. Plus, it would detract from Kess's show. And it would prove what Antonio had said all those years ago.

You're just a child, Anna.

She inhaled deeply and then looked Antonio straight in the eye.

"Could I request your assistance? Please," she added softly.

His lips quirked. "Other than rescuing a damsel in distress?"

It had been ten years since they'd last spoken. She thought she'd remembered his voice, but memories were nothing compared to the deep velvet that slid over her skin.

Steady. Now was not the time to be indulging in any kind of fantasy. Especially when she had a job to do.

"I need to get these heels off. Could you help me stand?"

Before she could stop him, he fisted his hand in the folds of her skirt and tugged up. Just to the middle of her calves, but the gesture froze her breath in her lungs. Her heart kicked into overdrive as his tan fingers slid over her ankles, undid the strap of the offending shoe with skilled dexterity, and slid it off. He repeated the same process with the other as she sat there like a child, barely keeping her mouth closed even as she wanted to release a sigh at how wonderful the brief grazes of his fingertips felt on her skin.

She should be embarrassed. Humiliated. Petrified as the cameras clicked on and the hum of audience gossip built like bees buzzing furiously.

But she didn't. All she felt, all she saw, was tied up in that moment.

"Thank you."

His eyes met hers and, for one second, she saw a mahogany fire flash within the depths.

Then it disappeared just as quickly as it had come. Whatever emotion she'd hoped she'd seen was probably nothing more than a reflection of the cameras capturing her literal fall from grace.

"Anna!"

She turned to see Kess approaching them.

"I'm getting back up." She shot her friend something that she hoped resembled a smile, aware that the world was watching every moment of her little drama. She started to shift on Antonio's lap and stand. A grunt escaped his lips.

"Oh! I'm sorry, did I hurt—"

He stood in one smooth motion, an arm wrapped around her back, the other holding her legs as he strode forward and set her on the catwalk.

"You can do this," Kess whispered from behind her as Anna stood. Anna glanced down at her friend then silently chastised herself as her eyes inadvertently drifted to Antonio. He stared at her for one long moment, his gaze opaque, before giving her a nod of silent encouragement.

Anna swallowed hard and turned to face the audience. Thunderous applause rose up, echoing through the plaza as people cheered. She forced a smile onto her face to acknowledge the support of the crowd, inclined her head and then started forward, holding up the skirt so she didn't have a repeat performance.

Despite the warm reception to her tumble, her eyes grew hot. For one blissful moment she'd been distracted by Antonio. But now, standing alone on stage with all eyes fixed on her, it was a struggle to finish her walk without giving in to the embarrassment that tightened her throat or the worry in the back of her mind that she'd sunk Kess's show.

And then there was the knowledge that as she reached the end of the runway and posed, Antonio was watching her.

You can do this.

Kess's words added fuel to the fire that started to burn low in her belly. She could do this. She raised her chin, aimed one last watery smile right at the cameras, then turned and walked back down the runway.

She saw him out of the corner of her eye, could feel his gaze pinned on her. But she stayed focused, looking neither right nor left, as she neared the end.

Antonio had helped her tonight; that much was true. She would have to send him a thank-you card or something to the Cabrera family home in Spain. But his one moment of kindness didn't change that he had taken her offered heart and cruelly shattered it. That he'd never once reached out in all the time they'd been apart. At one time, he had been her friend, her strength, her first love.

But that time had come and gone.

She passed by him, proud of herself for not giving in to the temptation to look at him. This time, she was the one who would get to walk away.

CHAPTER TWO

AN HOUR LATER, Anna sat facing the Trevi Fountain, arms crossed over her stomach as she stared up at the illuminated statues guarding the bubbling waters of the most famous fountain in the world. At nearly eleven o'clock at night, most of the crowds that had congregated to watch water flow from the historic landmark had disappeared, leaving her with a pleasant sensation of having the small plaza almost completely to herself.

After the show, Kess's firm had hosted a cocktail party. Anna had somehow made it through the hour-long event, her feet encased in flat sandals beneath the folds of her skirt. Judging by the praise she'd overheard Kess's boss bestowing on her, the fall hadn't negatively affected the show. If anything, it sounded like it was going to bring more attention to Kess, the featured designer, and Hampton Events.

After changing and wiping the layers of makeup off her face, Kess, who had turned the after-party over to her assistant, had invited her to walk to the Trevi Fountain. Kess's mom had called from Nigeria, so now she stood off to the side chatting about how her first show had gone, giving Anna time to just sit and breathe.

At first it had been blissful; the music of the water, the heat of the day giving way to the gentle warmth of an Italian summer evening. But the initial magic had dissipated, a fresh wave of embarrassment suffusing her limbs. Embarrassment and irritation that Antonio of all people had been the one to rescue her. What were the odds that she would not only fall at a fashion show, but fall into the arms of the man who'd rejected her so many years ago?

Her stomach rolled and she focused on the statue of Oceanus's nearly naked figure standing guard over the fountain. She was in *Rome*. Why ruminate on the past when she was in one of the most incredible cities on the planet? When just eight months ago she'd barely ventured out of Granada, let alone Spain? And now she was in front of one of the most iconic fountains known to man, letting her mind wander yet again to the city that had once seemed like her saving grace, only to turn into a prison.

Crossing her arms over her chest, she gazed out over the centuries-old architecture. The bearded, muscular statue of Oceanus presided over the masterpiece. Horses leapt out of stone on either side. Two nude male figures led the beasts, one trying to tame the wilder of the horses, the other raising a conch shell to his lips. Water splashed from beneath Oceanus's feet and tumbled down over three ledges before cascading into the massive pool filled with coins.

One coin tossed with your back to the fountain and you'll return to Rome.

She smiled. Kess had told her the legend on their walk to the fountain.

Two coins and you'll fall in love.

Antonio's face as she'd last seen it, youthful and yet so mature and serious at the tender age of nineteen, appeared in her mind.

Three coins and you'll be married soon.

Not a chance. She'd once dreamed of love, marriage, children. One day she'd circle back to that. But ever since she'd been let go from her job as a fashion buyer for a clothing retailer, she'd decided to finally stop existing and start living. The firing should have felt like a failure. But it had felt like a new beginning. Moving away from Granada, financing her own apartment in Paris for a year through a combination of her savings and a small inheritance, and finally picking back up the fashion design career she'd dreamed of in college. Granted, the portfolios she'd sent out the first half of the year had garnered almost no interest.

As angry as she was at Leo White, the fashion columnist, and how he'd used her, she did owe him one favor. He'd forced her to confront why her work wasn't getting any attention. The anger at how he'd used her had also uncovered confidence she hadn't even realized she possessed. Without his interference, the gold gown wouldn't exist and she would have never set foot on that catwalk.

Another glance at Kess confirmed she was still conversing with her mom.

The exhaustion spread, dragging Anna's shoulders down as she yawned. She'd flown into Rome last night, caught a few hours of sleep and dragged herself out of bed just after dawn. The thought of crawling into her cozy bed with its crisp sheets made her head droop.

But she wouldn't leave Kess. Not after everything she'd done for her. She'd been the first person since Antonio to push her, tell her she could achieve something on her own like switching her degree from generic business to the passion her mother had instilled in her with trips to thrift stores and dressing up at home. She hadn't recognized it at the time, but changing her degree against her aunt and uncle's strongly worded advice had been her first step toward moving away from their heavy influence.

Not that her uncle Diego or any of the others back at Casa de Cabrera had meant to be so controlling or to hurt her. Her uncle, especially. He'd gained a child while losing his beloved baby sister in that car accident. She knew that, as she'd grown, it had pained him to look at her sometimes.

When she glanced in the mirror, she saw her mother, just as he did.

A light breeze whispered across her skin. She looked up again, taking in the exquisitely carved detail of the statues, lit up by the warm glow of spotlights. The lullaby of dancing water soothed the tension brought on by her hectic day.

Her eyes dropped once more to the coins winking at her from the fountain floor.

"Legend says if you toss a coin into the fountain, you'll return to Rome one day."

Her body tensed. Time had deepened his voice into a richer timbre that resonated through every nerve ending in her body and rooted her to the stones beneath her feet. The chaos of earlier had dimmed the effect. But now she felt it, every intonation seeping deep into her bones with an intoxicating, delicious warmth.

A hand appeared in front of her, palm up, a coin resting on long fingers.

How many times had she held that hand as a child, clasping those fingers as he'd led the way up a mountain path or under the winding vines of the vineyard, offering her a respite from the suffocating confines of her adopted home?

Or the last time she'd seen him, when he'd pulled his hand back and walked away from her?

"Rome is beautiful," she replied, inwardly wincing at the breathiness in her voice. "But why go back to what you've already seen when the world has so much more to offer?"

For a moment, he said nothing. Then, with a casual flip of his fingers, the coin arced up into the night air before dropping into the water.

You can do this.

Steeling herself, she faced Antonio Cabrera for the second time that evening.

The butterflies returned with a vengeance, madly fluttering in her chest as her heartbeat raced. When he'd walked away from her, he'd been just shy of twenty, with a smile so sweet it had made her ache. But now...

Sexy. That was the best word to describe the tall, brooding man standing just a couple of feet away. A black suit, Armani label, judging by the cut and the glimpse she got of the unadorned silk lining. The material clung to his broad shoulders, customized for his muscular body. Even though he'd been shorter than his brothers, he still loomed over her. She should have kept her heels on. Then she wouldn't have to tilt her head back to meet his gaze.

His mahogany-brown gaze that ignited a spark deep inside her. One that burned brighter as her eyes slid over him, taking in both the familiar and the new. The familiar square jaw and sharp cheekbones, now dusted with dark stubble that should have looked scruffy but on him radiated roguish masculinity. The familiar chestnut hair, now trimmed on the sides and thick and wavy on top.

And his mouth. Familiar, but no longer gentle as it curved up into a smile. A sensual, brooding smile that fanned the flames burning inside her.

"Hello, Anna."

CHAPTER THREE

¡Dios mío!

Desire reared in his head, unbidden, unwanted, and dark with intensity as Antonio Cabrera watched Anna. *Anna Vega*, he reminded himself, an *A* and a *V* intertwined on the labels of her designs. He'd honed his skills over the past few years as head of Cabrera Properties, specifically their three luxury hotels. Negotiations, sales, the occasional ferreting out of an unsavory business partner. His reputation as tough but fair, an overall good man, had been hard fought.

What would his associates say if they could read his mind now? He'd thought his nineteen-year-old dream of Anna and him in bed had been bad; a dream that had been seceded days later by the fracturing of their friendship. But his adolescent fantasy was nothing compared to the want that had bolted through him when Anna had first stepped onto that runway in a gold gown with a skirt that shimmered like stars as she'd walked. Although the skirt had only held his attention for a second before his gaze had been drawn to the plunging neckline that almost reached her trim waist. Two panels of gauze had covered her breasts but left an enticing expanse of bare skin. The hint of a shy smile on her lips, painted a dusky pink, paired with a strength he'd never seen in the thrust of her shoulders and the tip of her chin, had upped the heat simmering in his veins.

The heat that had nearly spiraled out of control into a white-hot inferno when she'd landed in his lap.

He breathed in through his nose.

Off-limits. Old friend. Broke her heart. Virgin.

The reminders fell flat as he subtly flicked his eyes down her incredibly long legs. Anna Vega had grown into a stunning woman. Still slender but no longer the willow-thin wisp she'd been as a girl. No, he'd most definitely felt the curve of her hips, the nip of her waist when he'd briefly clasped her in his arms. Brown-black hair had grown down to her waist. The wide, rosy lips and those hypnotic eyes, one the rich color of amber, the other a pale blue.

Stunning. A sexiness he could have written off as mere attraction to a woman based on physical interest had she not gotten back up on the catwalk and finished her walk. He couldn't picture the old Anna facing the world after an embarrassing incident, let alone get up there in the first place. But this new Anna, the one who wore eye-popping gowns and modeled, was an entirely different and very enticing woman.

Diego had said nothing of modeling, he thought testily. Only that Anna's friend had talked her into showcasing her designs at a fashion show in Rome.

"I'm worried about her," Diego had said two days ago when he'd come into Antonio's office and asked for a favor. The wrinkles carved into his weathered face had deepened with his frown. "First, she lost her job. Then she ran off to Paris. And that magazine article that shared all her personal details..." His voice had trailed off, he'd inhaled deeply then pinned Antonio in place with a desperate gaze. "You said you'd be in Italy for a while. Would you check in on her? Make sure she's okay?"

Not his first choice of activities given how he and Anna had parted. He also didn't like that the butler apparently still treated Anna like a child. Diego's protective measures for Anna had rivaled that of Javier Cabrera and the restrictions he'd placed on his middle son, Alejandro.

But Diego had made a compelling argument. And it was the first thing the old butler had asked for in his thirty-plus years of service to the Cabrera family.

So he'd found out where Anna's friend's show was being held and secured a ticket. The company, Hampton Events, had checked out. So had Anna's friend, Kess. Still, he'd decided to watch the show, attend the after-party, confirm with his own eyes that Anna was okay before slipping away. She didn't even have to know he was there.

But then Anna had walked out on stage in that dress and he'd barely kept his mouth from dropping open. Each creation she'd worn, ones he'd read in the program had been designed by Anna herself, had shown just how much she'd grown into her woman's body. The first few had looked good on her, although they'd seemed fairly mundane.

But the gold gown...he hadn't been able to look away.

He'd convinced himself as he'd waited for her after the show that it was an anomaly, months of abstinence combined with the shock of seeing the "new" Anna. After the intensity of his reaction when she'd fallen into his arms, he'd been even more determined to see her; not just for old times' sake, but to see her in ordinary clothes, face scrubbed free of makeup, so his brain could let a certain part of his anatomy know she wasn't that stunning.

Bad idea.

Very bad, because Anna was even more beautiful without the dressings of couture. A lean face with sharp angles softened by wide lips and her gentle multicolored gaze presented an alluring contrast.

The last time he'd seen her, she'd been growing into the gangly limbs that had propelled her and her wild imagination through the vineyards year after year as he'd tried to keep up. Back then, she'd had to tilt her head back to meet his eyes. Now she stood just a few inches shorter than his own six-foot-two. The black jacket over a white T-shirt and slim jeans she wore should have looked casual. But the damned clothes drew his eye to the curves of her breasts and her long, long legs.

"I'm well."

Her abrupt answer snapped him out of his inappropriate perusal.

"Quite a different environment than Granada." He nodded toward the sparkling waters of the fountain.

"I bet you're used to glamorous destinations like this."

He frowned. She'd surprised him by not taking the coin he'd offered. The old Anna would have clutched it to her chest, closed her eyes, murmured a wish and tossed it into the fountain with glee. The rejection, small as it was, unsettled him.

Now you know what it feels like.

The nasty whisper inside his head deepened his frown. He had no reason to feel guilty about what had transpired between him and Anna the last time they'd spoken. None.

"I do travel a lot, yes. But apparently you

have, too. Diego mentioned you've been living in Paris?"

Her lips softened a fraction. "It's been fun."

The distance in her voice was very un-Anna-like. He also didn't like that she didn't take the bait, acknowledge that she'd been at Adrian and Everleigh's party. He'd seen her from the balcony, felt a prickle of awareness and looked up just in time to see her run away. Surprisingly, it had hurt. Growing up, and especially after Alejandro had been banished to England, Anna had been his best friend.

"Sorry I landed on your lap."

He waved the apology aside. "Not a planned event, I'm sure."

"No. What are you doing here?" she asked as she crossed her arms over her chest.

"One of my hotels is just a few blocks over. I know the owner of the Hotel dell'Orchidea. He offered me a ticket to tonight's event." The lie rolled off his tongue. "I wasn't expecting to see you on the runway."

She huffed. "I wasn't, either. My friend Kess is the producer of the show. A model got sick this afternoon, and I wanted Kess's first show to be a success." She glanced down at her feet, one hand drifting up to tuck a wisp of hair behind her ear. "I don't know if you've talked to my uncle recently, but I was let go from my job in Granada earlier this year."

"He mentioned it."

She bit down on her lower lip. "Yeah. Embarrassing for the girl who wanted to make a career in fashion."

He frowned. "From what your uncle said, the company was bought out and downsized your office. Nothing about your talent."

"I guess." She looked up but not at him. Her gaze drifted back to the fountain, her expression one of defeat. "I know that, logically. Stupid that it still kicked my pride."

Her dejected tone negated her agreement and thrust him back to the little girl who had appeared in the grand foyer of Casa de Cabrera seventeen years ago, newly orphaned, eyes downcast, and a pink suitcase clutched in her tiny hand like a lifeline.

He followed her line of sight to the fountain.

"Tell me what you see."

She glanced at him, a little V forming between her brows. "What?"

"I'm curious what you're seeing as a first-time visitor. Whenever I'm in Rome, I pass by the Trevi Fountain multiple times a day." He turned and pointed to the sandstone-colored towers of the Hotel de Cabrera standing proudly against the sky just beyond the plaza. "After a while, you get used to it." He stepped toward her. Satisfaction wound its way through him as he noted the flare in her gaze, the quick intake of breath.

What kind of a bastard did that make him? To reject her years ago, yet still thrill at the confirmation that she wasn't immune to him, at least physically? After the horrific night that had almost resulted in death, he'd tried to make amends and resume the mantle of the good son he'd worn so well during his teenage years, even if his parents didn't know what had happened.

His brothers did. They knew every sordid detail, which was why, after that night, he'd kept them at arm's length. He loved his brothers, respected them, appreciated their discretion and, when he'd needed it most, their support. But their knowing what he'd done, taking care of his mistakes and making sure that nothing was leaked by the hospital or the police, had made him withdraw.

In a way, his reverting to being "the good son" and making up for the effects their behavior had had on their parents in the ensuing years felt like repaying a debt. Adrian's distant coolness had hurt their mother, while Alejandro's misadventures had infuriated their father. Antonio's warm relationship with his mother and his respectable reputation had eased his parents' pain and taken the burden off his brothers. It had also felt justly like punishment. Why should he get to enjoy life when he'd nearly taken someone else's?

But apparently his body was tired of being the good son because right now the faint floral scent emanating from Anna's lush hair had him imagining her sprawled across the silk sheet of the Presidential Suite, her dark tendrils spread across a pillow as he slid the gold gown off her body.

"Tell me," he said again, managing to keep his voice even, "what do you see? What's it like to see the most famous fountain in the world for the first time?"

She watched him for a moment, eyes narrowed. Suspicion rolled off her in thick, palpable waves. He stared right back. He'd faced down furious hotel owners, greedy executives and, earlier in the summer, a very angry supermodel who couldn't understand why going through his phone would result in him sending her away from the Caribbean resort he'd whisked her to. He could most certainly face down his former best friend and, hopefully, yank her out of her melancholy state. It was the least he could do.

Although, the longer she stared at him, those colorful eyes glittering in the evening light, the more he wondered if he'd made a mistake. Anna had always seen what others hadn't. The hurt of Alejandro's absence. His anger at his father for taking away his brother. The helplessness at being unable to solve his mother's pain over Adrian's coldness.

What did she see now?

Finally, she turned away and faced the fountain. As the water splashed and the lights illuminated the centuries-old architecture, her shoulders relaxed.

"It's incredible."

She uttered the words in a breathy, sensuous voice. *Damn it*. But he'd started this game, goaded her into spinning a story just like she had when they'd traipsed around the Granada estate. A leaf carried on the wind had become a vessel carrying fairies to the nearby woods. A scuff mark in the dirt had been the result of a goblin being spooked from napping in the vineyards. Anna had lived in a world of make-believe. As a child, he'd found it enchanting. As a young man, it had been one of the many reasons that had convinced him that Anna was off-limits. She'd been so young, so sweet in her dreamy-eyed innocence.

"I can imagine all the people who have come here over the years," she continued, her eyes wide as she visually feasted on the sight before her. "Lovers in the eighteenth century stealing out at night to toss a coin in the fountain and share a kiss. A mother praying her son would come home from a war. An old man paying homage to his late wife." Her lips turned up into the first true smile he'd seen. "Remember all the fairy tales I read as a child? Perhaps at night the statues come to life and the horses gallop across the water." Her laugh electrified him, as bubbly as the water cascading down into the pool. "If I close my eyes, I can hear them." She turned to look at him and, upon meeting his stare, froze. Pink tinted her cheeks and she lowered her eyes, as if embarrassed. "Sorry. Probably not what a travel connoisseur like yourself would put in a guidebook."

He'd wanted to hear the old Anna. Be reminded of some of the happiest times of his life while also being reminded that this was *Anna*. Fashion designer, model, or whatever she'd become, she was an old friend, not a woman to be lusted after.

Unfortunately, as she'd spoken, he'd realized that while the old Anna who found magic in a sunset still existed, she'd grown up. Grown up and mixed that intoxicating magic with confidence that wove a spell so tight he could barely take a breath.

"You'd be surprised," he found himself saying. "Not what I'd put in a guidebook," he added with the slightest hint of a smile, "but an Instagram post or a review to share with our guests? Absolutely."

Her face lit up with joy once more as she grinned.

"Maybe I can translate telling tall tales into a career if my designs don't take off." She nodded in the direction of the hotel. "Kess's first time producing and the first time my designs have been on a runway."

"Is that what you've been doing since you moved to Paris? Designing?"

She nodded. "Not much success. Yet."

The desire to ask about the magazine article lingered on the tip of his tongue. When he'd read Leo White's description of Anna—*The niece of the Cabreras' long-time butler, an aspiring fashion designer with a love of fairy tales who's saving herself for her Prince Charming*—he'd been livid at such a private detail being aired to the world and…shocked. Intrigued. A tendril of lust he'd squelched as quickly as it had appeared.

"Who is Kess?" he asked. A much safer topic of conversation.

Anna gestured toward the far side of the fountain, where a tall black woman in a blue sundress stood chatting on the phone, although her gaze was trained on him and Anna. Even at this distance, he recognized the photos his private investigator had delivered in a thick folder, part of the dossier he'd put together.

"Kess Abiola?"

"Yes. We went to school together in Granada. Kind of cool knowing someone who actually made it in the industry and got hired by a big firm like Hampton. This is her first show, but she'll be booking big names within the year."

Antonio bit back a smile. Anna had always been a loyal friend. The pride for Kess rang strong in her voice.

"Although," she added, the brief sparkle of her expression dimming, "I guess you're probably used to rubbing elbows with the rich and famous."

"Alejandro, as you know, was much more drawn to supermodels and actresses and heiresses than I was."

"I saw he's engaged." Anna shuddered. "Hard to imagine the boy who put peanut butter in my sneakers and a fake spider in my coat pocket having a wife."

"Would you believe he's marrying a woman who's a straitlaced rule follower?"

Anna laughed, a sound that was as cheerful as it was deep and rich.

"I think I met her, actually, at Adrian and Everleigh's engagement party. She was very kind to me. And Adrian is married now, and expecting." Anna smiled. "Your mother must be thrilled."

"She is." Although the last time he'd seen his mother, just before journeying to Rome, she'd been unusually pensive for a woman who had gained two daughters-in-law who seemed to adore her.

"I saw you. At the engagement party."

Anna's eyes darted down.

"Did you? I didn't see you."

"Didn't you?" She looked up, startled, and he held her gaze. "I could have sworn when I looked out from the balcony you saw me and turned away."

She sighed.

"I didn't feel like having the first time we saw each other after..." Her voice trailed off and she waved a hand in the air. "The *incident* be at your brother's engagement party."

The Incident. She sounded almost disdainful when she said the words. He narrowed his eyes. She was physically attracted to him. And when she'd fallen into his arms, he could have sworn he'd seen the same emotion on her face that he'd seen when she'd told him she loved him.

Now...now he couldn't tell. Her blue-amber gaze was shuttered, her face still as if it had been carved from the same marble as the statues behind her.

"Anna."

Kess approached them, the sundress molded to her tall frame. So tall, in fact, that her dark green eyes were level with his.

"I didn't realize you had friends in Rome."

She stopped next to Anna, her eyes razor-sharp, her look of warning clear in its meaning. Anna was someone she cared about and if Antonio did anything to hurt her, she'd make him sorry.

He gave her a slight nod.

"This is Antonio. He's an old friend."

The producer extended her hand. "Kess."

"I know." He smiled as he accepted her hand, acknowledging her place in Anna's life and her subtle threat.

Kess stared at him a moment longer. Whatever she saw must have passed her test because she returned his smile.

"Ready to go back to the hotel?" Kess asked Anna.

Dismay settled heavily in his chest. He'd only

planned on stopping by to see the show and say hello, make sure she was handling the newfound publicity all right and then leave. But the evening had gone by in a flash, each moment whirring by so quickly, time had been like water in his hands.

That he wanted just a few more minutes in her company was indicator enough it was time for him to bid farewell and put as much distance between Anna and him as possible. He'd hurt her once in his quest to do the right thing. He wouldn't risk hurting her again.

That and, despite his brothers' obvious happiness, a long-term relationship wasn't in the cards for him. Most definitely not now, perhaps not ever. His career took him all over the world. With the addition of his collaboration with Alejandro on the floating hotel *La Reina* in Marseille, and future projects in the works, he had no time for a girlfriend, let alone a wife or children. Anna had spoken often of wanting to be a mother. As much as the thought of another man being with her—*touching her*—bothered him, someone else would have to give her the gifts of commitment and motherhood.

Even if he'd been interested in marriage, even if they'd both be able to get past the pain of their last encounter, he would never be able to trust himself to take a risk again.

And Anna was most definitely a risk.

"I don't know," Anna replied to Kess's question, drawing him out of his thoughts. "I'd thought about going to see the Spanish Steps."

"It can be crowded at night," Antonio interrupted.

"Is there a good time to go?"

"Dawn."

Anna scrunched up her nose. "Not my first choice of time. But I'll try."

"I hope you enjoy it." He glanced at his watch. "I have to get back to my hotel. Duty calls." An excuse, but a tried-and-true one. He nodded to Kess and then to Anna. "It was good to see you. I assume I'll see you at Alejandro's wedding in a couple of weeks."

She stared at him for a long moment, those eyes gleaming with something he couldn't quite decipher.

"Sorry again about earlier. Good to see you, too, Antonio."

He paused. He didn't like leaving things this way.

But you have to. He'd built his identity on his principles, on doing the right thing. Seducing his virginal childhood best friend whose heart he'd already broken once was most definitely the wrong thing. He would withdraw, take an ice-cold shower, and regroup in the morning. He'd fulfilled his promise to Diego, made sure Anna was all right. Now he needed to leave and let Anna live her life.

With that thought resonating in his mind, he walked away, leaving Anna and all the temptation she presented behind him.

CHAPTER FOUR

PINK RAYS OF early morning sun nudged the remaining shadows of night aside and bathed the ancient buildings of Rome in a rosy glow.

Beautiful. Anna wrapped her arms around her middle and breathed in. All her life she'd dreamed of traveling to places like this. Especially in the last five years as her friends from university had left Granada for bigger and better things while she'd returned night after night to the same yellow bedroom with its white chintz curtains and twin bed. Still stuck in the past. Stuck in the confines of her uncle's fears. Stuck in her own.

But no more.

She passed by a bakery, the doors thrown open, golden light falling on the stones outside the shop and freshly baked rosemary bread scenting the air. One of the few businesses open before sunrise. A bird flitted past. Violet flowers spilled from an urn. The only signs of life on the otherwise empty cobblestone streets.

Amazing, she thought with a little thrill, that

she was in one of the most visited places in the world and yet felt like she had the entire city to herself.

She turned a corner and stopped in her tracks. Some of her joy dissipated as she read the black lettering emblazoned over the glass doors of a tall building sprawled across the entire front of the plaza she'd just walked into.

Hotel de Cabrera.

"Of course," she muttered.

Italian flags framed the doors on either side. Perfectly arranged sconce lights created intricate diamond patterns on the cream-colored stones. Most of the arched windows were covered by burgundy curtains. Although, as she looked up to the top floor, one curtain twitched then was drawn aside. A woman in black lingerie stood in the window, framed like a seductive painting as she gazed confidently out over the plaza. A man appeared behind her, pressed a lingering kiss to her neck as she smiled and then the curtain fell back over the window.

What would it be like to have that kind of confidence? To look out over the world with such assurance?

Granted, she'd surprised herself with her own strength the last few months. Although, she acknowledged irritably, yesterday's bravado when faced with her first love had not come effortlessly. She'd had to make multiple mental trips into the past, summoning up the hot flush of shame that had swept over her when Antonio had stared at her like she'd grown an extra head and not just confessed her love at the tender age of seventeen. Or the freezing sting of rejection that had rooted her in place when he'd walked away.

Amazing how fresh the hurt felt after all these years. But it had done its job yesterday; helped her keep her distance even though her heart had been pounding so hard the beat had echoed in her ears.

He is attractive, she reminded herself as she resumed her trek across the plaza. *Perfectly reasonable reaction.*

Well, not just attractive. More like sexy as hell. She'd been in such a rush to hide at Adrian and Everleigh's engagement party that she'd only caught a glimpse of his dark handsomeness. And when she'd fallen yesterday, her flustered mind had latched onto two details: the deep, dark brown of his eyes and his rich, woodsy scent that had momentarily stolen her voice.

But when they'd talked by the Trevi Fountain, she'd had the opportunity to see him, truly see him, for the first time since their parting at the vineyards in Granada. His strong jaw, fierce lines still evident beneath his dark beard. The boyish smile she'd remembered so fondly replaced by a brooding smirk that had chased away her girlhood dreams and replaced them with dark, sensual fantasies. Fantasies that included Antonio's masculine arms wrapped around her as he lowered his mouth to hers....

As if her naughty musings had summoned him, there he was, striding out of the doors of the hotel. Dressed in tan slacks and a forest-green polo that fit his muscular chest to perfection, he looked far too awake and professional for such an early hour as he scrolled through his phone.

The confidence that had empowered her last night took one look at Antonio in all his handsome glory, turned and fled, leaving her in the middle of the plaza with nothing but her old insecurities and self-doubt. His attention was fixed on his phone. If she quickened her pace and kept her head down, she could reach the other side before he—

"Anna?"

Too late.

She forced herself to stop and smile casually at him, even though the closer he drew, the faster the butterfly wings in her stomach beat until she felt like her entire body fluttered.

"*Buongiorno*, Antonio."

He arched a brow as he stopped a few feet away. She remembered his older brother, Adrian, doing that when he'd found them in the vineyards stuffing themselves with grapes. On him, it had looked arrogant and stuffy. On Antonio, it looked masculine and sensual.

"You're up early."

"You said the best viewing of the Steps was at dawn." She nodded toward the burgeoning glow above the rooftops. "It's almost here."

He glanced over his shoulder then back at her, chocolate eyes dark and unreadable.

"That's the only reason you're here?"

She frowned. "Why else would I be?"

He stared at her a moment longer before flashing her the tiniest smile.

"I'm going with you."

For a moment, she just gazed at him, the words not making sense.

"Go with me?" she repeated.

"To the Spanish Steps."

Her pulse kicked into overdrive as she blinked at him like a deer caught in the glare of headlights. Conflict raged inside her chest. More time spent in his company was risky given the roller coaster of emotions she'd been riding since last night. Not to mention all the opportunities it created for her to stick her foot in her mouth. Her rational mind listed off these reasons even as temptation whispered for her to seize what Antonio offered.

Say no. Say no.

"Why?"

A frown clouded his face. Most women probably said yes to anything he asked without a second thought. She hadn't sought out information about him but that hadn't stopped pictures gracing the covers of magazines, or popping up on Instagram from time to time, of Antonio occasionally in front of one of his resorts or at some high-profile meeting, and once in a while with his arm securely around the waist of a gorgeous actress or heiress to such-and-such a business empire.

Each picture had been a stab to her heart. Over time, those stabs had become less painful, more of a quick, dull ache. Except now the images paraded through her mind, ripping the Band-Aids off her wounds and flooding her with fresh pain.

She must be a glutton for punishment to even consider spending time with him when all he'd brought her the last ten years was hurt.

"I haven't seen the Spanish Steps in a long time. I haven't seen you in even longer."

"You saw me last night."

"For five minutes."

"And then you left," she retorted, unexpected irritation hardening her voice. She didn't get angry. Anger hadn't been a part of her idyllic childhood before the car accident that had claimed her parents' lives. After she'd been sent from the sultry wet heat of Louisiana's bayous to the dry, arid slopes of the Sierra Nevada mountains to live with her uncle Diego and aunt Lonita, she'd quickly learned that anything other than a demure smile sent her new family into a tailspin. Tears led to more restrictions to keep her safe from sadness. Ire led to caution about the dangers of going too far down the path of anger...followed by more restrictions.

Safety had become synonymous with repression. Diego's fear of losing his sister's daughter had colored his decisions on everything from the friends she spent time with outside of school to where she went to university. He had always stepped in, taking care of things for her, encouraging her to ask for help, ask for help, always ask for help, never feel like she had to do anything alone.

Sometimes she asked for help because she knew if she attempted something on her own, it would frighten him. Other times, even when she thought herself capable, a fear had sprouted up inside her, a fear that the reason everyone was always offering to help her, to watch out for her, was that she really couldn't do it on her own. She still felt that fear, felt that pervasive intrusion at the worst possible moments.

Perhaps it was the absence of fear that had allowed her frustration at Antonio's sudden about-face to come through. Because there was nothing to fear, she realized. Yes, she'd had an adolescent crush at him at one point. A part of her would always care for him. At one point, he'd been her best friend, the only person in her life who'd believed her capable of more.

But the worst had already happened. He'd rejected her. She'd dealt with the pain. She'd gotten a degree in fashion, made friends, moved to Paris.

And now… She raised her chin. She was going after her dream. Whether she and Antonio parted ways now or spent an hour in each other's company, it wouldn't change all she'd accomplished on her own.

Or that, after today, aside from Alejandro and Calandra's wedding, she probably wouldn't see Antonio again.

The ache pulsing in her chest dimmed a little as elation spread through her. She *could* do this. She could act like a mature adult, sightsee with an old friend and then say goodbye. And if his departure hurt a little, she'd been through worse and survived.

"All right."

"Don't sound too excited," he replied dryly.

A small smile tugged at her lips. "I am excited to see the Steps."

His low chuckle stirred a warmth in her belly. He stepped forward, took her hand in his and tucked it into the crook of his arm.

Relax. Enjoy the moment.

With that mantra playing on Repeat in her head, she flashed a smile up at Antonio and moved forward. The sun was rising, she was in one of the oldest cities in the world, and a very handsome and very famous billionaire was escorting her through the streets.

Antonio played the perfect tour guide, pointing out the history of a random building here or a random statue there. At first, she enjoyed it; the deepness of his voice, the heat of his arm beneath her hand, the magic of Rome.

But every now and then something about his tone unsettled her. Commanding, self-assured in his knowledge, yet distant. An occasional glance confirmed that his face was smooth, almost devoid of expression. The teasing glint she'd glimpsed last night when she'd fallen off the stage, the whimsical offer of a coin to toss in the fountain, were absent, replaced by a mysterious man she didn't know.

The thought dimmed some of her excitement. He reminded her of his older brother, Adrian. A little more personable but restrained, in control. Granted, he was in charge of two European luxury hotels, a hotel in the Caribbean and a real estate firm with properties around the world. Being intimidating was probably a billionaire requirement.

It didn't take away some of the nostalgic sadness for the boy with a kind smile and a deep soul who had been her friend, her protector and eventually her love. Come to think of it, she'd noticed that distance in him before yesterday. The one and only other time she'd seen him in the last ten years, at the party in Paris. She'd remembered him being happy, carefree, almost worshipping of his brothers back in Granada. But that day, even though she'd seen him congratulating Adrian on the balcony, there had been something reserved in his manner.

Whatever had happened to Antonio had affected more than just their friendship. Curiosity and sadness trickled through her.

"Everything all right?"

She looked up into his handsome face. Eyes the color of molten dark chocolate, thick brows drawn into a slight frown. She'd once been able to tell him everything. She'd taken a leap last night when she'd gotten back up on the catwalk. What if she took another leap now? Asked what had happened, what had changed him?

"Anna?"

"Fine," she responded brightly. What was the point in pushing? She didn't know the man escorting her through Rome. She knew who he used to be. But what would it accomplish to ask an intimate question when in an hour or two he'd once again be out of her life?

His lips parted, probably to pursue. He'd been the one person Uncle Diego had trusted her with. Would Diego have allowed the friendship had he known that Antonio pushed her, encouraged her? The adventures he'd planned, from wandering the streets of Granada after school to exploring the mountain slopes, had reinvigorated her joy for life after her parents' deaths. He'd drawn her out of the armor everyone else had built to keep her safe, dismantling it piece by piece, then done the unthinkable; handed her the reins to fix whatever obstacle she'd been facing, from bullies at school to what she wanted to do after graduation. It had been empowering. Strengthening.

It had made her fall in love with him.

She looked away, searching for something, anything, to distract him.

"Oh!"

The exclamation that burst from her lips was authentic. A stone boat sat in the middle of the street, partially sunk below the cobblestones. The boat lay in a small pool, water trailing over the sides and out the bow and stern. A smaller fountain stood in the middle of the boat, shedding water into its belly.

"I didn't even know this existed," she breathed as they drew closer. "I can't believe it's just sitting in the middle of the road."

"It's suffered damage here and there."

"I'd never have guessed with how perfect it looks. What's it called?"

"Fontana della Barcaccia. Fountain of the Leaky Boat."

She laughed. "Descriptive."

The corner of his mouth quirked. "Legend has it that when the city flooded in 1598, a boat was left in this exact spot when the waters receded."

"What a lovely piece of lore." Her eyes moved past him and settled on the Spanish Steps climbing up to the Trinità dei Monti, the crosses of the church's two towers standing tall against the backdrop of a few puffy clouds drifting lazily across the sky. Terra-cotta pots overflowing with bright pink flowers were artfully placed all over the staircase.

"I don't know which is more beautiful," Anna said with another laugh as she darted around the fountain and started for the stairs. She bounced up the first flight, giddiness and anticipation filling her with every step. She stopped at the first landing and spun around, her smile so wide it almost hurt, but she couldn't stop it even if she'd wanted to as she breathed Rome in. The gentle fragrance of the flowers surrounding her, the soft hum of conversation as more people moved into the plaza and ascended the Steps, the warmth of the sun on her back as it climbed higher into the sky. Somewhere, a musician started to play an accordion, the rich, reedy melody adding the perfect festive touch to an already perfect scene.

And Antonio. Against all odds, she was sharing this incredible moment with someone who had been a dear friend, her fellow adventurer. She smiled down at him...

For a moment she thought a cloud had moved over the sun as the plaza dimmed. Goose bumps pebbled on her skin. Antonio was staring at her, standing on the bottom step, eyes narrowed, jaw tight and expression almost cold. A look she'd seen once before, an expression of disdain.

She crossed her arms over her stomach. She knew what would come next…unless she left before he could reject her again.

Had she truly thought she could handle the pain she'd known was waiting at the end? She should have told him no outside the hotel, walked away with her head held high instead of setting herself up for this.

She swallowed hard and hurried back along the steps.

"Sorry, got caught up in the moment. It's starting to get busy." Her lips began to ache they were stretched so tight into an overly bright smile "It was nice to see you, Antonio. I have to get back, we're supposed to leave by—"

"Anna." He stepped in front of her and blocked her path.

She inhaled deeply to steady herself, but all it did was fill her with the scent of him.

You can do this.

She'd faced down a runway full of professional models, a crowd of the crème de la crème of European society, and an ex-best friend. She'd gotten back up after she'd fallen, both figuratively and literally.

She squared her shoulders and raised her eyes to meet his.

His gaze hardened. She took a step back as uncertainty whispered through her. He took her arm and she gasped as his fingers circled her wrist, firm and warm, like they had been last night when he'd so deftly removed her heels. Gone were her teenage fantasies of a chaste kiss on the lips. Instead, her innocent dreams had been replaced by the deep, dark desire to feel his hard, muscular body against hers.

"Anna," he repeated, and she jolted, her cheeks heating.

"Yes?"

"We need to talk."

CHAPTER FIVE

ANNA'S EYES WIDENED. Judging by how he'd tried to rush off, she'd probably been expecting some form of rejection. Not that Antonio could blame her. When she'd spun around on the Steps, he'd been captivated. He hadn't been able to discern which shone brighter, the sunlight that backlit her body or the smile on her face. It had sparked a cascade of memories, of how much Anna had enjoyed anything and everything with a joy he'd experienced just by being around her and seeing the world through her eyes.

He knew as soon as he'd seen her in the plaza this morning that he should have said hello and continued on. Dealt with the other matter by email or a phone call. Something where they weren't in close physical proximity.

But, his conscience had argued, that was the coward's way out. This needed to be dealt with in person. So he'd placed himself in his own private hell as he'd escorted her, her hand tucked into the crook of his arm making heat simmer in his blood. The initial touch had burned like hot silk gliding over his skin. He'd managed to quell his subsequent lust by recalling the article Alejandro had gleefully texted him at two in the morning.

He'd wondered when he'd seen her outside the hotel if she'd seen it, had been waiting for him to talk or even seek out the comfort of an old friend. He never would have thought he'd be playing her knight in shining armor once more, but here they were, twice in less than twenty-four hours, at the mercy of the gossip-hungry media.

Unease rippled through him. Would they dig up what had happened? What he'd spent the past ten years trying to atone for? The one night he'd slipped, tried to indulge in a bit of illicit fun, for which his best friend had nearly paid the ultimate price. It had confirmed that taking personal risks wasn't something he could afford to do. Especially when he had the guilt of William's brush with death and the humiliation of both his brothers having to come to his recue constantly lurking in the background of everything he did.

He'd put everyone at arm's length since that night. William. His brothers. Anna. He'd always been the "good son" growing up, but after the accident, he'd sought out, and achieved, perfection. The perfect son, the perfect student, the perfect CEO. His mother's sadness over her lack of a relationship with her oldest son had been assuaged by her youngest's achievements. His own aspirations of translating his enjoyment of travel had been transformed into a career when his father had handed him control of Cabrera Properties and the opening of the French Riviera hotel because of his stellar academics and internship with the family's hotels in London, his successes mollifying the effects of Alejandro's antics on their sire. He was generous to those who demonstrated loyalty and definitive in cutting those who weren't out of his life and his business. And now his holdings, especially his three hotels, were thriving because of his leadership, with a fourth hotel in the works. A unique property that, when successful, would be another notch in his professional portfolio.

He enjoyed women, too. Not as much of a monk as Adrian, but not as much of a libertine as Alejandro. Conversation, companionship, and good sex coupled with discretion made for the best relationships. If any one of those factors were missing, he ended it, swiftly and usually generously.

A well-ordered life. Predictable, more luxurious than he deserved, yet controlled. One that had been upset with the media's suddenly obsessive attention on the older Cabrera brothers both getting engaged so quickly. The mania surrounding his family had reached new heights as reporters had turned their eye on him, wondering who would catch "the last Cabrera bachelor." It had reached a fever pitch in the weeks following Adrian and Everleigh's wedding in New York. Reporters camped out on the sidewalk across from his hotels, trying to get a photo of whomever he might be escorting home after a date. The last time someone had been bold enough to approach him directly, he'd brushed them off with a bland, "Who I'm seeing is none of your concern." That reporter had run with a story that Antonio *was* dating someone, leading to a new feeding frenzy of discovering who had captured the youngest Cabrera's heart.

This article, no doubt one of many in the pipeline after Anna's landing in his lap, was only going to make it worse. Not only were the papers gleefully declaring that they had uncovered his secret girlfriend, but he hadn't been able to get her out of his mind since last night. Usually, nightmares plagued his evenings. Waking up drenched in sweat to the echoes of glass breaking and metal screeching was not unusual.

But last night… No, last night when he'd woken, it had been to blood pounding through his veins and vivid images of Anna splayed across his bed. That was why, when she'd spun around, eyes full of dreams and her thousand-watt smile aimed right at him, he'd been furious with himself. He'd told himself he'd escorted her so they could talk about the article. But it had been selfish motivation that had made him offer to walk her, not a desire to help. He'd wanted more time in her company, to bask in the happiness she created and savor time with the beautiful, confident young woman she'd grown into.

A flash cut him off before he could speak. He turned in time to see a wiry young man with sunglasses and a baseball cap pulled down low streak across the plaza, a camera clutched in his hand.

"Maldito."

The oath escaped as the wind caught the photographer's hat and lifted it off his head. The man slowed, glanced back… And quickened his pace into a sprint when he realized he was in the crosshairs of Antonio's furious gaze.

Antonio crossed the plaza in several quick strides, his legs eating up the distance. He plucked the ball cap off the cobblestones and made a mental note of the logo emblazoned on the front before throwing it in a nearby trashcan.

"We need to get out of sight," he said as he crossed back to Anna. He reached out, grabbed her hand and dragged her along the stairs.

"Antonio, what—"

"Now, Anna."

For a moment, she hesitated. Then she fell silent and allowed him to pull her down the Steps, across the stones and into a narrow alley. Greenery-filled terra-cotta pots lined the street as vines twisted their way up walls. Aside from the waiter sleepily draping white cloths over tables outside a café, the neighborhood was empty.

"Where are we?"

"The Via Margutta. An artistic quarter."

"This is from *Roman Holiday*!"

He tempered his fury as Anna pulled away and walked a few steps down the alley. She obviously hadn't seen the article, didn't understand the implications of a photographer following them and snapping their photo this early in the morning. Let her have a few more moments of bliss before he yanked the rug out from under her.

He gritted his teeth. He'd grown up with the media scrutinizing his every move. He knew the importance in addressing potentially harmful news. Since she'd arrived in Spain, Anna had grown up in a bubble. As much as he respected Diego, he hadn't understood the obsession with keeping Anna locked down so tightly. Anyone could have seen how miserable she was at being so restrained.

And yet, as he watched her look around the alley in wide-eyed wonder, he felt a moment of kinship with the family's butler. In that moment he wanted to keep her safe, bundle her back to Granada before a reporter climbed up the drainpipe outside her hotel to sneak a picture of her getting out of the shower or stalked her all over town.

Determination settled in his bones. By showing up last night, he'd done more harm than good. He was responsible for this, so it was up to him to fix it.

"Gregory Peck's character lived on this street. A

reporter," she said as she looked up, eyes fixed on the windows above them. "Started out scummy, but ended very sweetly."

"Unfortunately, most reporters don't undergo such a dramatic character revision," Antonio replied dryly. "I have evidence of that."

"So do I." She frowned, a frustrated huff escaping her lips. "Did you see the magazine article?"

He paused then answered truthfully. "Yes."

She closed her eyes for a moment, then opened them, pinning him with that arresting amber-blue gaze.

"He spoke to me at Alejandro and Everleigh's party." She huffed again and tucked a strand of loose hair behind her ear. "At first I was…flattered. He asked about the dress I was wearing, one I designed."

"How did he find out…" He let his voice trail off, one eyebrow going up suggestively. Cool, collected. Even though he was anything but on the inside.

She grimaced. "Because I'm an idiot. He made a raunchy joke, I replied I wouldn't know because I'd barely even been kissed. He lasered in on my comment like a sniper. Asked if I was waiting for Prince Charming. I got flustered and said 'Something like that.'"

More hair fell out of the loose bun on top of her head. A messy style that should have looked frazzled, but on her looked carefree an, like she'd just rolled out of bed. She probably had, he realized, an image of her in bed in nothing but a negligee flaring in his mind.

She sighed, brushed the hair behind her ears again in a gesture that reawakened a memory of her scampering up a hillside, perching atop a boulder and smiling down at him, cheeky and barefoot and innocent.

Innocent.

The word burst through his illicit daydreams.

"You would think," she said, continuing on with no clue as to what debauchery his mind had just entertained, "that a mention in a top fashion magazine would be everything an aspiring designer could want. But the inquiries I've gotten haven't been about my work. Well, hardly," she amended as she started fiddling with her bun, tugging and pulling loose strands up through the band. "Most have been about your family, inside information on Adrian and Alejandro. Do I know who you're dating…blah-blah-blah." She yanked so hard on one strand of hair, he nearly winced on her behalf. "Leo White made me sound like a naïve goof. No respectable brand is taking me seriously— they just remember that I'm 'the aspiring virgin designer.'"

Her head snapped up at the sound of his snort. "What?"

"Did someone actually say that to you?"

"Yes. And don't you laugh," she retorted with

a fire that intrigued him. The old Anna had never stood up for herself. "The couple of portfolio requests haven't gone past a 'thanks for sending this.'" She shook her head, the strands she'd just put in place falling once more to form a halo of dark brown around her face. "Although that's my own fault."

"How so?"

Another shake, dislodging more hair. "Long story. A problem for me to fix."

Her words caught his attention. At the age of ten, she'd been more than happy to let him take the reins, rely on him. With the void of Alejandro's company, he'd welcomed the role of not only friend but protector.

But the resolve he'd glimpsed last night was apparently not a fleeting thing.

"Besides," she continued, "most of the people who contacted me are just trying to use me to get to your family."

She shuddered, wrapping her arms around herself as if trying to ward off some unseen enemy. The result of the sudden shove headfirst into the world of the rich and famous.

That meant that what he had to show her next wasn't going to make things any better.

She suddenly gave him a sweet smile tinged with embarrassment. "Sorry. All this time and I'm still using you as a sounding board for my problems." She closed the distance between them and, before he could guess what she was about, went up on tiptoe and kissed his cheek. The simple gesture tugged at his heart. "It was nice catching up, Antonio. Thanks for showing me the fountain and the Steps."

Get it over with.

He pulled his phone out of his pocket, clicked on the link Alejandro had texted him, and handed it to her. She accepted the phone with a quizzical look. Then her eyes focused on the glaring headline and her lips parted.

For several long moments, the only sounds were the scrape of table legs as the waiter continued to set up the café and the soft coos of a couple of pigeons dancing around his feet in hope of scraps. He gazed around the street even as he kept Anna's face in his peripheral vision. Her expression was surprisingly hard to read. He'd expected trembling lips, perhaps even a few tears or a full-on collapse into crying. But she surprised him, her face unexpectedly smooth except for a tiny little V between her brows as she read.

Although, he reminded himself, Anna had truly changed since he'd seen her last. The Anna of his childhood would have turned crimson and run off after falling off the catwalk. She had blushed last night, but she'd gotten back up, and done so without a single tear. He admired her for that.

Finally, she looked up. She didn't say anything, just stared at him with wide eyes.

"*Sí*, Anna. We have a problem."

Anna looked back at the phone then slowly read out loud. *"'The Virgin and the Billionaire?'"*

The headline burst off the screen, splayed across the page in large block letters. But even worse was the picture beneath—a photo of Anna splayed across Antonio's lap, the gold gauze of her skirt hiked up past her knees to showcase her bare legs. Her eyes were locked on Antonio's face, lips parted, arms wrapped around his neck. His gaze was fixed on her, one arm curled possessively around her back as the audience around them stared in openmouthed glee at the drama unfolding just feet away.

Alejandro had thought it was hilarious. Adrian had yet to reach out. Neither had his parents or Diego.

A small sigh escaped Anna's lips. "I don't see how this is newsworthy."

Her irritated tone made him suppress a grin. He was enjoying the feisty version of Anna far too much.

"Apparently, a slow news day."

"And what kind of title is that?" She looked up, her eyes sparking with a fire that made him grit his teeth at the desire it reignited. "It sounds like a lurid romance novel."

He nodded at the picture. "It does look like the covers of the books you see for sale at the airport."

She looked back down. Her cheeks pinked. "Yes, well…"

His lips quirked. "You read them, don't you?"

She paused a moment then raised her chin and shot him a smile. "I do." She handed the phone back to him. "I'm sorry, Antonio. Truly." She looked at her feet, the gesture more reminiscent of the Anna he'd known. "I can't believe that one stupid shoe has caused all this trouble."

He cleared his throat. "Yes, well, the damage is done. Now we just have to decide what to do about it."

CHAPTER SIX

ANNA BIT BACK a groan. The image of her body inelegantly splayed across Antonio's lap with that horrible title, written all in caps, would forever be burned into her brain. She looked ridiculous. Like one of those perpetually stunned heroines on the covers of a gothic romance running across a cliff in her frilly nightgown toward a dark castle. Antonio, on the other hand, oozed confidence and sexuality, as if a woman hadn't just landed in his lap.

"Maybe it'll go away in a day or two?" she finally managed to say.

"I'd hoped for the same when Alejandro texted me." He pulled up something else and handed it back to her. Her stomach dropped. Tweet after tweet accosted her, along with her name and the photo underneath Twitter's "What's Happening" column.

She'd been turned into an international joke in less than twelve hours.

"I'm sorry," she repeated, her eyes sweeping over

the cobblestones, the planter on the stoop just to her right, her own feet. Anything but him.

"It's fine, Anna."

He didn't sound fine. He sounded tense, frustrated. That was understandable. From what Uncle Diego had said when he and Aunt Lonita had visited her in Paris last month—a visit where Diego had spent part of the time installing new locks on the doors and windows while Lonita had piled food into her cupboards and asked not so subtle questions about the crime rate in the surrounding neighborhood—Antonio had become notoriously secretive about his personal life. He was respected and admired in both his professional and social circles. Landing on the cover of a global tabloid was most likely at the bottom of the list of what he considered respectable media coverage.

He shifted in front of her, drawing her eyes from her own feet to his polished leather shoes. She frowned. There had been a time when he'd run wild across the slopes of the Sierra Nevada with her, his feet bare and covered in mud as they'd climbed trees and scaled boulders.

What had happened to that carefree, adventurous soul? She'd loved that about him; the tap of a pebble at her window or a note slipped under her door, inviting her on an afternoon of adventure. The times she'd felt free, felt like she was truly herself, had been those afternoons spent barreling through fields of wildflowers or splashing in a nearby creek. The girl who disappeared into grief and fear that she wasn't capable, wasn't strong enough, was truly too fragile to accomplish anything on her own, had morphed into someone strong, someone daring and exciting, with Antonio. It was one of the reasons she'd fallen for him.

But from what she could see, if there was any trace of that adventure left, Antonio had buried it very, very deep.

"Not exactly the coverage either of us needed," she finally croaked.

Not to mention the humiliation of Antonio knowing she was still a virgin. She didn't really care if anyone else knew. But Antonio knowing... she bit back a sigh.

"Walk me through the last few months of your life."

Antonio's command surprised her. "What?"

"If we're going to make a decision on how best to handle this, I need more information."

"Since when do you ask for more information? I remember you diving headfirst into everything."

His jaw tightened as his eyes glittered. She suppressed a shiver. Something had happened to Antonio, something dark, to make him look so forbidding.

"I know you lost your job. Start there."

The bald statement made her flinch. If he noticed, he didn't care. *Fine*, she thought with not a small degree of anger. The harsher he was, the easier it was to push away her physical attraction to him.

"After I graduated, I landed a job with a clothing retail chain based out of Granada. They were bought up earlier this year by some American company and downsized our office." She frowned. "It wasn't my dream job. I suspected they used factories that weren't employing the best labor practices."

"A common theme in fashion."

"It shouldn't be," she shot back. "If I ever get a chance to sell my designs, I'll make sure the manufacturers are sustainable and ethical."

He tilted his head to the side. "A noble goal. Then Paris?"

"Yes. Kess challenged me to take a year off, put together a few portfolios and see what I could accomplish. I moved to Paris in the spring, before Adrian and Everleigh's engagement party. A short-term rental on a flat." A flat with curling wallpaper, a leaky faucet that only seemed to drip once she was in bed, and a wrought-iron balcony that sagged away from the brick exterior. But it was cheap. No point in running through her inheritance and her savings just in case she needed it later. Plus, the top floor boasted the most incredible floor-to-ceiling windows that lit up the room she'd claimed as her studio. She swam in swathes of fabric and scribbled designs, sipping on coffee in the morning and red wine at night.

It was the first time she had truly been happy in years.

"You said almost no requests on your work since the article?"

She shrugged. "Some. None that went anywhere. The companies I submitted to on my own…" Her face flamed as she remembered the video chat with a sour-faced woman whose lips had pinched together as she'd rapidly clicked through Anna's submission on her laptop and referred to Anna as the "virgin designer." "They're not taking me seriously after the way Leo made me sound. It's going to take work to get past that."

As much as she wanted to blame Leo for all her misfortunes, the hard truth was, all of her work up until the gold gown had been inspired by other people's ideas. Even in college, she'd recreated the gowns of her favorite princesses and heroines. Not once had she made something original.

It was going to take work. But it was time to take the risk and get out of her own damn way.

Amazing how at the beginning of the year moving to Paris had seemed like a mountain in itself with what she was facing now.

"What about the show?"

"I might get some inquiries about the gold gown. But I need to create a stronger portfolio, and soon," she added with a wrinkle of her nose. "Strike soon while this show is still fresh in people's minds."

Antonio stepped forward, his shoes drawing closer to her flip-flops. He placed a finger under her chin. Her breath caught as he slowly raised her face. She wanted to pull away, but that would show her hand, how much his touch affected her physically.

Or did he already know what effect he caused? The desire to slip her hand into his like she used to when they were kids, to feel his palm against hers? But now, as an adult, to imagine his hands sliding down her body, settling on her waist with the same possessive touch he'd shown when he'd pulled her down the Steps and into the Via Margutta?

"Why did I have to pry all of that out of you?" His voice came out low and warm. "You once used to confide in me."

"As did you to me. Guess that makes us even."

The words had tumbled out before she could stop them. She blinked in surprise at her own audacity. When was the last time she had challenged Antonio? Never, if memory served. She had talked his ear off as a child, as if all the words she'd kept to herself in her uncle's house bubbled up at once and flowed forth. But as the years had passed and Antonio had grown from gangly youth into a strapping young man with dark hair that tumbled down to his rock-hewn jaw, she'd talked less. She hadn't wanted to tax him, to risk driving him away, when he had so many other things to occupy his time, more interesting people to see. Like his other friend William and all the girls at school who had fawned over him.

Now she just didn't care. In fact, driving him away was sounding better and better. If it wasn't his know-it-all attitude driving her nuts, it was how damned handsome he looked in that polo.

He ran away last time. Just say the L-word again and watch how fast he runs.

She stepped back and, thankfully, his hand fell to his side.

"I didn't mean to drag you into this. It's my problem to deal with."

He arched a brow and held up the phone, the sight of the picture making her wince. "You didn't really drag me in. You fell on me."

She rolled her eyes. "Thanks for the reminder."

"It's a problem for both of us. Although, if anyone is to blame here, aside from the press, it's whoever manufactured that shoe."

The comment startled a laugh out of her. "Fair." She rubbed at the bridge of her nose as a headache started to build. "Look, I'm headed back to Paris for the rest of the year. I'll be far away from you—" *thank God* "—so no more paparazzi photos. We won't be together. This whole mess will die down." She sucked in a breath. "Even if the designing doesn't go the way I want it to and the press bug me for a bit, it'll die down once they realize they made a mistake."

"Or we could pretend to date."

CHAPTER SEVEN

ANNA STARED AT him as if he'd just announced his decision to give away his fortune and go live in a hut on the beach. Given their history, she had every right to question his sanity. But his solution was a viable one. Being seen on his arm would catapult Anna from magazine footnote to international star. Brands would be clamoring for her portfolios. And he would get the damned picture-snapping fools off his back.

"What… I don't even know how to respond to that."

Jazz music filtered out of the café speakers as the waiter placed a chalkboard sign on the street advertising their menu.

"Let's grab a coffee and I'll explain."

Anna stared at him for a moment longer before tentatively following him to the café. The waiter seated them and, after taking their order, disappeared inside.

"You need to get the attention on you refocused."

"Need is a strong word. I'd like to, but—"

"You just said you didn't like the direction your career was heading. As much as I despise articles and photos like this, it's giving you an opportunity to change that direction."

She frowned. "Doesn't pretending to be your girlfriend keep the attention on who I know?"

"At first, yes. And the first week we give them exactly what they want. Photos of us holding hands, going on dates. Brands are either not focusing on your work at all or won't take you seriously."

"Yes, but my work could be better. I—"

He took his phone out of his pocket, pulled the article up and slid the phone across the table. Anna put her hand over the screen.

"Seeing it once was more than enough."

"What better way to get rid of the naïve label than by dating one of the world's richest men?" He motioned to the text beneath the photo. "The story has written itself. We act it out and change the way people see you. Wear some of your designs when we're seen together. Your work starts getting international attention."

She bit down on her lower lip. "So we pretend to be a couple for a few weeks and then...what? Fake breakup?"

"Yes."

Her teeth dug deeper into her lip. It dawned on him that his offer could be perceived as cruel. She'd poured out her heart to him once, imagining herself in love with her best friend, only to have him rip away the blinders of innocence and cut off contact.

Now here he was, offering to pretend and give her a shadow of what she had wanted all those years ago.

Not the same. They were both adults now. She hadn't given any indication that she still harbored feelings for him. A thought that should be a relief but instead bothered him, a persistent scratch on his skin he couldn't quite shake.

The waiter came out and set two steaming cups and cannoli on the table, the ricotta cheese cream spilling out from either end of the fried pastries. Anna swiped a bit of filling and slid a finger into her mouth.

"Mmm. That's really good."

He looked away and focused on the wrought-iron balcony two stories up on the other side of the street. "It is."

"What do you get out of this?"

Thankfully, by the time he turned back, she was holding her cup.

"A couple of things. One, we would start off the charade in Positano, which is the site of my newest hotel. The media will follow, especially after that incident this morning in front of the Steps. They'll take photos of you with your new boyfriend, and at some point someone will casually mention my newest hotel or even get a photo of us there together."

"Free advertising."

"Yes."

She nodded once, her eyes fixed on the foamy top of her cappuccino. Did she think him a bastard for taking such a mercenary approach to the arrangement? If she did, it was probably a good thing. Better for her to think of him as cold than to entertain any possibility of something real happening between them.

"And the second thing?"

"I'm grateful for the happiness my brothers have found." Even if he did experience the odd occasional pang of envy. "But marriage is not in my future. The tabloids haven't stopped following me around since Alejandro and Calandra's wedding this summer. They aren't focusing on Cabrera Properties or the new hotel, just who I'm dating."

"Is something wrong between you and your brothers?"

"No. Why?"

She took another sip of her cappuccino. "You seemed…distant at the engagement party."

Warning whispered across the back of his neck. Not once in ten years had anyone commented on the change in his relationship with his brothers. HWas this wise, being around someone who had once known him almost better than he'd known himself? Who still picked up on details no one else did?

Bile rose in his throat, thick and bitter. What if she found out what he'd done? What he was capable of?

Before he could explore that thought, a figure paused at the end of the alley. Even from this distance, he could see the camera in their hands. Irritation and resolve wiped away his concerns. He needed to get the media off his back.

"It was a busy day, that's all. Back to my proposal. We'll start today, and I'll make the arrangements up through Alejandro's wedding."

Anna frowned. "I haven't said yes yet."

But you will. He smiled at her. A slow, sensual smile he'd used on women who'd captured his interest over the years.

"What can I say to persuade you?"

She didn't even bat an eye. Instead of swooning, her frown deepened. "You said you want to get the media off your back about who you're dating. But isn't that what this whole arrangement will do? Put the focus on who you're seeing and not your new property?"

Her lack of response rankled him. But he maintained a neutral expression as he dove into the negotiation.

"Initially, yes. But it will refocus the narrative from who I might be dating to who I am supposedly dating. Every time I go out with a woman, the media splashes photos everywhere, publishes everything they can find on my companion." Irritation stirred in his gut. "Not the best way to conduct business with flashbulbs going off every time you meet with someone of the opposite sex. Their husbands and lovers aren't fans of seeing their names tied to mine along with the words 'rumored affair.'" One such article had severely threatened a business relationship he'd cultivated for years. "And as an added insult, the coverage of my new hotel has been spotty at best. At any rate, it'll lessen the scrutiny I've been under."

"This just seems a little farfetched."

Antonio shrugged. "Unusual, yes, but it's not implausible. Even if we published a statement saying we're not dating, they won't listen. If we take control of the narrative now, we can influence the outcome."

"Do we tell your family what's really going on? Mine?"

Maldito, he hadn't thought of Diego. The butler liked him. How would he feel about this sudden change from checking in on his niece to supposedly dating her? "I won't tell my family the real reason, no. Your uncle, though—"

"He's always liked you. Even said once he thought we would…" She shook her head. "As long as we don't recreate some of Alejandro's more sensational public acts, I don't think he'll be breathing down my neck about who I'm dating."

His hands curled around his cup. He didn't like the thought of her dating anyone.

"So that's a yes?"

She sighed. "I don't know."

He leaned in. "You could take back your life, Anna. You'll be staying in a luxury hotel with time to build your portfolio. Once this is over, you'll have designs to send out and the reputation to get a contract."

Devious? Yes. But how could she not see that this was the solution she needed? Yes, he would get the benefit of finally doing something for her instead of hurting her. Redirecting the media attention was another bonus.

As long as he kept his hands and fantasies to himself, it was perfect.

She stared at him for a long moment.

Then sighed. "All right."

Her resigned tone crawled across his skin. "All right?"

"Let's do it."

"Don't sound so excited."

"I'm not sure it's going to work. And you have to admit, it's weird that we went from best friends to…" Her voice trailed off for a moment and she focused her attention back on her coffee. "To not, followed by years of no contact, and then in twelve hours we make international headlines and dive into a fake relationship so the media gets off your back and I can try to get my career on track. Doesn't that all sound a little crazy to you?"

A smile tugged at his lips as excitement tingled in his chest. "It does. But I haven't done crazy in a long time."

CHAPTER EIGHT

"This is a bad idea," Anna repeated for the seventh time as wrought-iron gates parted to reveal a stone-paved drive.

"You mentioned that." She could hear Kess's grin through the phone. "I think it's exactly what you need."

"Yeah, sure."

The car started forward. The driveway sloped upward, the stones glowing beneath the lanterns that marched up to the imposing mansion in the distance.

Le Porto. The Haven. Antonio's boutique hotel for the wealthiest people in the world. The one that their little charade would place in the spotlight. It had stung, hearing that he had no problem pretending to be in love, or at least in lust, with her to get free publicity.

But, as he'd pointed out several times, she was getting something out of it, too. So why didn't she feel more excited, hopeful?

She leaned her head against the cool glass of the

window and stared out over the darkening ocean to her right. Probably because it still didn't sit well with her that she was doing exactly what some of those fame-hungry brands had tried to do—use the Cabrera name to advance themselves.

After she'd signed her soul over to the devil himself, Antonio had insisted on escorting her back to her hotel. She'd let him, walking in a daze as he'd rattled off a list of details. His car would pick her up at the airport. He'd meet her in Positano, where they would discuss a strategy for the upcoming week.

By the time he'd deposited her on the steps of her hotel, the sun had climbed into the sky and crowds of tourists were swelling in the streets. Kess had found her fumbling with her key out in the hall, taken one look at her face and followed her inside, where she'd gently but firmly demanded an explanation for Anna's shell-shocked expression.

Perhaps it had been the roller coaster of emotions she'd been riding since last night. Or maybe she'd been too tired to put up a fight. Whatever the reason, she'd let Kess guide her out to the balcony overlooking a quiet garden and press another cup of coffee into her hands. Kess had barely sat down before the whole story had come pouring out.

Kess, bless her, had just sat and listened. Nearly fifteen minutes later, Anna had finally run out of steam and drooped in her chair. She'd covered it all. The young boy who had befriended an orphaned girl newly arrived in a strange country. How free she had felt with her best friend when everyone else around her had suppressed her, creating a foundation of emotion that had evolved, as she'd grown older, into affection and then her first love. How she'd finally mustered up the courage to tell him how she felt his first summer back from college, only to have him tell her he'd never be able to see her as more than a little sister.

And how she had now done the most foolish thing of her life and agreed to be in a fake relationship with the man who'd broken her teenage heart.

Unfortunately, Kess hadn't uttered words of caution or talked her out of it. No, she'd been *thrilled,* encouraged the charade. Then she'd hugged Anna, said all the things a best friend would, and made Anna promise to text daily updates. Ten minutes after Kess had left, the front desk had rung to say that her limo had arrived. She'd almost laughed. *Her* limo? She hadn't missed the photographers clustered on the sidewalk opposite the hotel.

When she'd arrived at the airport, it had been to find that Antonio had stepped in once more and swapped out the ticket she'd managed to snag on her favorite airline for one of his family's private jets for the short flight to Naples, where yet another limo had awaited. She'd called Kess as soon as the limo pulled onto the winding road that led to Positano.

To her fake boyfriend.

"You know what you have to do, right?"

"Um…call and tell him I changed my mind?"

"No. Seduce him."

"Kess, he has no interest in me like that, even now," she protested, even though her heart flip-flopped at the word *seduce*. The woman in the hotel window materialized in her mind. She hadn't needed to see the details of her face to know she was the kind of woman men lusted after. Even if she wasn't a classic beauty or a femme fatale, her poise alone attracted men like moths to a flame.

A passing lantern threw her reflection onto the window of the limo. Plain brown hair pulled into a ponytail. Freckles on her nose. A swipe of mascara, a dash of tinted lip balm and she looked…the same. She wasn't unattractive, but she wasn't the kind of beauty men like Antonio and his brothers escorted. Everleigh Cabrera was a jaw-dropping blonde who sparkled. Calandra, whom Anna had only met once at the party in Paris, had had a bewitching dark vibe, aloof and mysterious yet surprisingly kind.

Her stomach dropped. Who on earth would believe that a Cabrera would date someone like her?

"The way he was looking at you last night by the fountain—"

"I appreciate the support, but you're wrong," Anna said firmly. "This is just business."

She said goodbye to Kess and watched the mansion grow closer.

You're getting a leg up in your career, she reminded herself, even if the thought of getting her big break because of her "romantic" connections and not her talent tied her up in knots. *You get to stay here. In a seaside Italian mansion.*

The intermittent changes of her travels had helped keep her mind off what was waiting for her at the end of her journey. Until now, that is, as the magnificent three-story mansion came into sharper view. The exterior was painted a seashell pink, so soft it was almost white, yet it glowed like a jewel as the last rays of the setting sun bathed it with an ethereal light. Balconies dotted the top two floors, and it looked like the right side of the mansion boasted a much larger balcony overlooking the sea. Columns covered in ivy provided privacy.

Pride surged past her trepidation. Antonio had shared how he wanted to make a career out of traveling. As much as she'd missed him when he'd traveled with his mom and brothers, she knew those had been some of the happiest times of his life.

The car pulled around the circular drive and stopped. On one side stood a three-tiered stone fountain, bone-dry and surrounded by an empty garden bed. Not what she had expected to see, but based on the articles Kess had texted her, the hotel was scheduled to open next month. On the other side, stone steps rose up to a double set of glass doors.

Scrolling through the stories had also confirmed what Antonio had said. The four articles Kess had sent gossiped about Adrian's recent wedding, Alejandro's upcoming nuptials, or speculated on Antonio's mystery girlfriend. The few snippets about the actual hotel quickly deviated to rumors like where Alejandro and Calandra would spend their honeymoon.

She swallowed hard. She had never once envied the scrutiny the Cabrera family lived under. Now, entering into this arrangement with Antonio, she was inviting the same kind of examination into her own life.

Despite her complicated relationship with her aunt and uncle, she'd texted them. Told them the lie of how she'd reconnected with Antonio unexpectedly in Rome and they were going to spend a couple weeks together catching up. As overbearing as they'd been, she still loved them. They deserved to hear at least something from her instead of seeing it in the news.

Their response had been surprisingly mundane. Her aunt had wished her a good time. Her uncle had simply said he liked Antonio and was glad they had reconnected. No third degree. No background checks like the poor boy she'd gone on two dates with in college who had angrily broken things off with her in the hallway of their dormitory when he'd learned a private detective had been calling around asking questions about him.

Was it possible they were finally letting go? Trusting her to make her own decisions? The thought of having finally earned their trust, overcoming their fears with her own smart decision-making, had been cathartic.

The limo stopped and the driver got out, moving around to open the door for her like she was a queen. Her courage evaporated. The tightness in her chest returned and twisted even further as she sucked in a shuddering breath. This was supposed to be fun, a harmless pretense and brief sojourn into luxury.

Instead, as the driver helped her out of the back seat, the sound of the limo door closing echoed in her mind with the clanging of a prison gate slamming shut. Before she could crawl back into the limo, the doors of the hotel swung open to reveal Antonio.

He walked down the steps, confidence rolling off his broad shoulders that had somehow been stuffed into a deceptively simple white T-shirt that probably cost the same as one of the evening gowns she'd put together last week.

His fingers closed over hers and she bit back a sigh at how wonderful his skin felt on hers, warm and firm. She looked up at him, prepared to say hello…and nearly yelped when he wrapped his arms around her waist and pulled her against him.

"Welcome, *tesoro*," he said as he kissed her temple.

Oh, no…oh, no…oh, no. What had she done? How could she possibly have agreed to this?

"Tesoro?" she managed to croak.

"It means 'darling'in Italian."

Luckily, she had put her arms around his torso in response to being hauled against him because her knees went weak at hearing his words.

"Good thing Kess isn't here."

He frowned. "Why?"

"She'd make something out of our deal. Kess was convinced you were attracted to me when we were talking by the fountain. Which is ridiculous," she babbled. "I know you weren't, but she's a die-hard romantic and wants to believe that everyone is going to find love—"

Antonio put a finger to her lips. "Anna. It's going to be okay."

The urge to nip the pad of his finger pressed to her mouth was too tempting. She turned her head away. Between the naughty images that had run through her mind last night and her sexy dreams, she had a darker side that craved much more than a kiss on the forehead from Antonio Cabrera.

Deep breath. Okay, she was insanely attracted to him. But she wasn't going to do what Kess had suggested. Business. This was a business arrangement.

"I appreciate everything you're doing, Antonio."

"You just don't think it's going to work?"

"Um…"

Antonio leaned down, his beard scraping gently against her cheek. She closed her eyes and inhaled. A mistake, as the intoxicatingly masculine scent of his cologne filled her.

"On the beach below is a photographer with a long-range lens. He's been hiding down there for nearly an hour and, I'm guessing, right now is busy clicking away."

Anna started to rear back, but Antonio kept her locked against his body.

"It's already working." He pulled away, a smug smile on his handsome face.

"But how did they know…" Her voice trailed off. "You called the media."

His grin turned even cockier. "I didn't. But some strategic phone calls from my secretary in Rome may have hinted at a possible change in plans for the beautiful woman who landed in my lap last night."

She couldn't help it; she laughed.

He winked. The small gesture twisted her heart, reminding her of the boy who had been such an incredible friend in her darkest hour. Was he still there, behind this cool façade?

"Once we get inside, we can further discuss our plans."

"Yes, sir," she responded with a salute. "Do you have maps? Intel on the reporters?"

He cast a suspicious glance her way as he led her inside. "Were you always this feisty and I just missed it?"

"No. I think I…"

Anna's mouth dropped open as they walked into the hotel. She took in the marble floor made up of swirling whites and creams, the pale colors and soft peach-colored walls glowing beneath the stunning chandelier hanging from the two-story ceiling. A white desk dominated the back wall, framed between two pots overflowing with bougainvillea. A magnificent staircase on either side of the room led up to a balcony overlooking the foyer.

"Antonio," she breathed, "this is magnificent."

"Signor Cabrera?"

Anna looked up as a tall, tanned man with an elaborately stylized moustache, wearing khaki slacks and a white polo, appeared on the balcony.

"Yes, Paul?"

"Shall I escort Signorina Vega to the room?"

"No, thank you. I'll show her myself."

Excitement danced up her spine. If the lobby alone was this fantastic, she could only imagine what the rooms looked like.

"Which room will I be staying in?"

Antonio looked at her, his face smoothing out until it was the unreadable mask he'd sported last night.

"Mine."

CHAPTER NINE

ANTONIO WATCHED AS Anna drifted to the edge of the balcony, her hands settling on the railing as she gazed out over the sea. She looked toward the reddish glow on the horizon, her profile in stark relief against the deep blue waves turning black.

He was a masochist to torture himself like this. When he'd suggested the idea of a fake relationship, it had seemed like a brilliant solution to both their problems. And when he'd spied the photographer on the beach, he'd seized the opportunity to kick off their charade. What better way to start the articles rolling than to be spied welcoming his paramour to his private hotel?

Yet when he'd pulled Anna into his arms, the alarm bells that had been dinging softly in his mind trilled into a full-blown cacophony. His blood had roared as his arms had closed around her tall, slender frame.

His hands fisted. He thought through everything with razor precision. His first property, a stunning resort in the French Riviera, had been on the verge of collapse when his father had tasked him with saving it. Visits to his competitors, frank conversations with numerous luxury travelers he'd wined and dined in the finest restaurants across Europe and, finally, a cohesive plan that addressed everything from room renovations to grounds-keeping to marketing, had led to profits in the first year that had impressed even his Javier. His subsequent successes had followed the same pattern, from burgeoning commercial real estate sales that he'd turned over to trusted parties last year to his ultimate pride. His hotels.

When he followed the rules, he achieved success.

But with Anna, he'd thrown all those rules out the window. He'd made a split-second decision that morning. Had he thought it through, he would have put more guidelines in place for how they would conduct their farce. Or he would have carried out a more accurate analysis of his physical response to Anna and realized the payoff wasn't worth it.

She moved closer to one of the pillars and tilted her head up and closed her eyes as she breathed in the scent of wisteria clinging to the column before walking back to the doorway that led into his chambers. Her gaze roamed over the room.

"It's not what I would expect for a billionaire businessman," she finally said.

"Oh?"

She walked deeper into the room. His chest tightened as she neared the bed.

"It's…cozier." She sat on the chaise longue in front of the bed and nodded in the direction of the fireplace. The architect had replicated Antonio's vision perfectly, mounting it in stone that stood proudly from floor to ceiling, while the glass provided a window into the sitting room beyond.

"This hotel is different than my others. With only having twenty rooms, including this penthouse, it provides more intimacy and exclusivity for my guests."

"And why am I sharing this room with you when there are nineteen empty ones?"

"To keep up the pretense."

She frowned. "For who?"

"The construction workers. The employees with the interior design firm. Anyone other than Paul."

The frown deepened. "I don't remember you being so suspicious."

"In my line of work, I have to be. A freckle-faced waitress could turn out to be a corporate spy from another hospitality chain. Or a vendor who schedules a meeting with me could be trying to get the layout of my office so they can break in and try to access my computer. Both have happened, by the way," he added with a nonchalance he didn't quite feel.

It had been unnerving to be thrust out of the bubble of security he'd enjoyed in Granada to the cutthroat world of reality when he'd entered the halls of Cambridge. He didn't keep friends, partially because of the past, but also because the people he came across in the outside world seemed to care more about his money than him. He dated casually but selectively. When the relationship moved further into intimacy, he'd taken Adrian's recommendation of having background checks performed or only dating women who moved in the same social circles as he did. It had kept his reputation intact, a professional necessity. As much as he might look back on his freer past in Granada with nostalgic longing, his current method was safer, logical.

If he occasionally felt the urge to resist the confines he'd set in place for himself, too bad. What right did he have to enjoy life when he'd nearly taken it from someone else?

"People can be cruel," Anna said as she stood up and moved to the fireplace. She ran a hand along the nearly black wood of the mantel. "Although they can be kind. Alejandro's wife was very kind to me at the party in Paris."

"She's a special kind of woman to be able to put up with Alejandro," Antonio replied dryly. "But then again, so is Everleigh to put up with Adrian's musty old soul."

Anna's lips twitched. "An apt description." She continued to walk around, her footsteps muffled by the thick rug between the fireplace and the chaise longue. "There are good people in the world."

"There are. There are also bad people. You trusted Leo White. Look what happened. The real world is a far nastier place than the vineyards back home."

Her shoulders slumped. "That's true." A self-derisive laugh escaped. "I was so naïve thinking that I could break into designing on my work alone. Like you said, it's who you know."

He suddenly found himself wishing the world was a gentler place, a place that didn't gobble up people like Anna and leave them hardened.

"You mentioned a long story about why your designs aren't being picked up?"

"Yeah."

She drifted away from him, walked into the sitting room. He followed at a distance, hands in his pockets. She sat on the low-slung leather couch, resting her chin in one hand as she gazed at the empty grate.

"You saw the article."

He leaned against the wall, nodded once.

"At first I was embarrassed that I had been duped and shared something so personal. I sounded like a five-year-old wanting to play dress-up." She sat back and scrubbed her hands over her face. "He didn't want to talk about my work. Just wanted dirt on people for his puff piece on the 'engagement party of the summer.'"

The face she made and the snobby accent she affected as she quoted Leo's article made him press his lips together to repress his laughter.

"But then…" The room grew so quiet, he could hear the slight whisper of her breathing as she inhaled. "I looked at what I was wearing."

He frowned. "What you were wearing?"

"At the party."

In his mind's eyes, he recalled the picture that had been posted next to Anna's biography.

"Pale blue dress, right?"

She nodded, her face sad. The urge to cross to her, pull her into his arms and soothe away the pain made him lean harder against the wall. He'd comforted her once before as a friend. But his role had changed drastically. He didn't trust himself not to take things too far in the confines of his private suite.

One hand moved back and forth over the buttery leather, her fingertips tapping out a nervous beat.

"When I saw the dress, it hit me. I used to think I was inspired by the fairy-tale movies my mother and I used to watch together. But I wasn't designing anything new." She flopped back against the cushions, the drooping of her limbs speaking to her personal sense of defeat. "Plain. Uninspired. Been done before. Nothing that was me."

The admission sounded torn from some deep dark place.

"You're being hard on yourself."

"Those aren't my words. Those are some of the comments on the portfolios I submitted before the engagement party."

Anger burned low in his stomach. He'd said similar things, and much harsher sentiments, in his career. Yet to hear that Anna had been subjugated to such bald and unforgiving commentary made him livid.

"Anna—"

She held up a hand. "Don't make excuses. When I saw that dress, saw how similar it was to another design, it hit me. After I moved to Granada, I was so sheltered, so repressed, I could barely breathe sometimes. And yet… I let my aunt and uncle take care of me."

"You were ten and you'd just lost your parents. Of course you should have let your family take care of you."

"But I didn't even fight it!" Frustration suffused her tone as she stood and started to pace. "I just let them treat me like a little girl for years. I'm twenty-seven now, and I just moved out on my own for the first time eight months ago. I didn't do anything on my own, including my designs."

Maldito, he could no longer take it, seeing her beat herself up like this. He crossed the room and stopped a few feet away, far enough to not touch her, but close enough to make his point.

"What about the gold dress?"

Her lips quirked. "The one I was wearing when I fell on you?"

"*Sí.*"

Pride brought her mouth up into a tentative smile. "It's actually the first dress I did after the party. I reworked and reworked it so many times, afraid each draft was just another replica, but…"

"It was beautiful, Anna."

She nodded, happiness brightening her eyes. "Thank you. It was, wasn't it?"

Amazing, the strength in this woman who had been through so much and, when confronted with the publication of intimate details that would have made women of his acquaintance run for the hills, had instead reflected on how she could improve and seized the opportunity with both hands.

Her body was sexy. But her confidence, her determination…that was alluring in an entirely different and very dangerous way.

Before he could pursue the topic further, she shook her head.

"Sorry. How did I even start talking about that?" She plowed ahead before he could get a word in. "What's the plan with this whole charade?"

He stepped back, putting both physical and emotional space between them. He wanted to know more, dig deeper. A sure sign that he needed to accept the chance to refocus on the business aspect of their arrangement.

"A few sojourns into town. Chances to be seen, photographed. A lunch here, a dinner there. Two weeks that will culminate in us being seen as an official couple at Alejandro and Calandra's wedding in Marseille. I was thinking we could start off light tomorrow with a lunch at a seaside bistro."

Something about their conversation had made her nervous. It was evident in her fingers tapping against her thighs, the tension in her neck.

"Something wrong?"

"What happened outside, the way you hugged me…is that going to be a regular thing?"

"Couples who are dating tend to hug and hold hands, yes."

"You kissed me on the forehead," she said almost accusingly.

The temptation to tease her proved too much to resist. "Would you have rather I kissed you somewhere else?"

She flushed and looked away, giving him a delicious view of her neck, the slightly gaping V of her dress that hinted at the curves of her breasts, barely visible in the dim light.

"I'm just wondering how much physical demonstration is going to be required."

"Some, Anna, but I'm not going to force you."

"I know that." Her gaze swung back around, narrowed and almost irritated. "I would never think that of you, Antonio." She blew out a breath.

"It's probably just me, then. Our parting was an embarrassing experience for me. I feel like it's lingering on the edge of my interactions with you."

He shrugged. "You were seventeen, Anna. You were young and you had a crush."

He waited for her to correct him. Rationally knew that when she didn't correct his use of the word *had*, he should be relieved.

Except he wasn't. The sting of knowing she no longer cared about him was poetic justice for the pain he'd inflicted on her. It would make it easier for him to carry out the pretense of being in a relationship.

"So we'll leave tomorrow. We'll have lunch. Then…two weeks?"

"Yes." Two weeks was good. Two weeks was enough time to sell the idea of a couple escaping to a romantic hideaway, followed by a few weeks of them disappearing off the media radar following the wedding. Gradually, the interest would die down. Anna and he would part ways, he without a bull's-eye on his back from the media and she with newfound attention on her designs.

Neat, planned-out and detailed. Just the way it should be.

She nodded once. "Two weeks. Got it." She glanced around. "Are there sheets or something for the couch?"

"You're not sleeping on the couch."

"I'm not taking your bed."

He leaned forward. "It's not a request. I will take the couch, and if you try to take it, I'll dump you on the floor."

Her mouth dropped open. "That sounds like the exact opposite of the chivalrous act of offering me your bed to sleep in."

"Take it or leave it. I shoved you into the pool how many times? Rolling you onto the floor is nothing."

The reminder of their old camaraderie made her smile despite her best efforts to keep glowering at him.

"Fine. Tonight. But we'll rotate. I'm not going to have you pretend to be my boyfriend and give up your bed the whole time we're doing this."

She stood and walked past him toward the balcony, leaving that damned floral scent in her wake. He sat back in his chair and scrubbed a hand over his face. It was going to be a very long two weeks.

CHAPTER TEN

ANTONIO GLANCED AT the form reclining on the balcony for about the sixth time since she'd walked outside and lowered her incredible body onto the chaise longue. Knowing that she had no comprehension of how sensual she looked, dark hair spread over the pillow and the skirt of that damned sundress riding up to expose a hint of her thighs, made it even more erotic.

He refocused on his laptop, his fingers tapping out a rhythm across the keys. The latest reports on two of his three properties were positive. The third, his resort in the Caribbean, was in need of a new manager after his last had made the unfortunate decision to sleep with the wife of a powerful guest. The first and last time he had trusted someone other than himself to make a critical hiring decision. Fortunately, the guest was also a longtime friend and had agreed to keep the matter quiet, especially in light of how his divorce had become a public spectacle.

Yet another example of why marriage had never

been on his radar. As a youth, his parents' union had been unappealing at best, no matter how much Isabella had tried to portray their marriage as a love match. The few times their father, Javier, had mentioned heirs to inherit the Cabrera business empire, Alejandro had reminded Antonio that that lovely duty fell to the oldest.

Antonio smirked. Funny how his wayward brother had fallen victim to the trap of matrimony and parenthood. The way he talked about his new bride, as if she were God's gift to womanhood, was in stark contrast to this time last year when he'd been running through girlfriends faster than Antonio could blink.

Although, both he and Adrian had seemed very happy the last time he'd seen them at Fox Vineyards in New York following Adrian's wedding to Everleigh. Even though he hadn't been emotionally close with his brothers in years, ever since he'd graduated from college and taken hold of Cabrera Properties, he'd formed a bond with Adrian and Alejandro built on respect and their shared successes. But instead of discussing strategies, Adrian and Alejandro had talked of pregnancy symptoms, first-anniversary gift plans and the years-long wait for an exclusive preschool.

His brothers had both been averse to marriage. What had changed their minds so drastically?

Anna shifted onto her side, propping her body

up on one elbow as she thumbed through a book. The new position made the bodice of her top gape.

He punched out a sentence on his computer, focusing on the clicking of the keys and not the delectable body of the woman just a few dozen feet away. His phone dinged. A screenshot from Adrian of the news story and a single-character text message: ?

Trust Adrian to keep his communication abrupt and to the point.

He scrubbed a hand over his face. It wasn't just the temptation Anna presented that had him questioning what he'd set in motion. In his mind, he'd estimated entertaining this fake relationship for no more than two weeks. Long enough to give the illusion that he was seeing someone exclusively, followed by a few months of him lying low, and the media would go after someone else.

Yet what would happen when Adrian's and Alejandro's wives gave birth? When the media realized that he and Anna were no longer an "item"?

He pinched the bridge of his nose. He hadn't thought this through. Not beyond the initial idea of getting the media off his back *now* and giving Anna's career a boost. Although he could admit the latter reason had formed more out of guilt than a desire to help. Guilt had been a powerful motivator for him these last ten years. It had kept him in line, kept his education and then his business on the fast track to success.

But this time guilt had propelled him into making a hasty decision.

Too late for another option. Yes, it was. Even if it didn't solve his long-term problem, at least he would get a break for a few months and repay Anna for the heartbreak he'd caused her.

Although she was certainly paying him back in her own way. That she didn't know it, made it even worse. Even as he watched out of the corner of his eye, she ran a hand through those long, silken tresses, strands of dark hair falling forward to caress the column of her neck.

"Antonio?"

The sound of his name tumbling off her lips yanked his mind out of the gutter. He blinked and focused on her.

"Yes?"

Anna had sat up and was now watching him with a concerned look on her face. "Are you all right?"

"Yes. Why?"

"You look angry."

He smoothed his expression. "Apologies. Just thinking."

She stood and walked toward the door, leaning casually against the doorframe with her arms wrapped around her middle. In the blue-and-white-striped shorts and loose white tank she'd changed into for a moonlit walk on the beach where they'd held hands and pretended not to notice the photographers further down, she looked like any other woman he might have spied around Positano.

Except she wasn't just any other woman. She was his former best friend, the person he'd trusted more than anyone else still . And now little Anna was gone, replaced by Anna Vega, stunningly beautiful and yet still sweet and innocent, it made him feel like a first-rate bastard even thinking about her the way he did.

"Thinking about what?"

"Business," he replied shortly as he turned back to his computer.

"I don't believe you."

His gaze snapped up. Anna's eyes were pinned on him, roaming over his face like a hot caress that could see past all the defenses he'd built up.

"Why not?"

"Because I know you." She cocked her head to one side. "Something's bugging you."

"If I feel the need to share, I will."

His words came out colder than he'd intended, but they elicited the desired effect. Anna reared back as if she'd been slapped, stared at him for one long moment then turned and walked back onto the balcony. She grabbed her book off the chaise and disappeared around the corner.

Good. When she was in view, she was too much distraction. While everything seemed to be lining up for the grand opening, his attention needed to be focused on that.

Except it wasn't. It was on that damned scent—*her* scent—lurking on the air. The feistiness in her voice, the vulnerability she'd shared with him. The vivid image of her amber-blue eyes widening in pain before she'd walked away. Not with the flamboyant flair of drama his Caribbean lover had exhibited. Not with tears pouring down her cheeks like the opera singer he'd seen last summer. No, she'd walked away with quiet dignity and grace.

Damn it.

He stood and stalked to the balcony door. A glance to the right confirmed that Anna had sought refuge at the far end. But instead of sitting on the bench built into the wall or cozying up in one of the plush chairs he'd had brought in from Paris, she'd chosen to perch on the edge of the balcony railing, one bare foot resting on the tile and the other on the railing. His body tightened as he stalked toward her.

"That's a long drop down."

She didn't even look at him, just kept her back to him as she gazed out over the sea, the sky appearing starless behind the bright white of the moon. "Yes. Good thing there's a railing here."

"Railings are fallible."

For a moment, there was nothing other than the faint roar of the ocean. Then, so quiet he barely heard it, a dejected sigh.

"I remember a time when you played, Antonio. Barefoot. In the rain."

He remembered the last time he'd done that. He remembered that day all too well. It was the day he'd no longer seen Anna as a friend and little sister. The summer after his first year at university, just a week away from flying back to England, Anna had insisted on taking him out for a picnic she'd packed. A picnic decimated by an unexpected rainstorm. Instead of running for shelter, Anna had kicked off her shoes and jumped in the fast-forming puddles. Antonio had joined her, indulging in one last bit of childhood.

Until she'd spun around, wet hair clinging to her face, a stunning smile on her lips, and white shirt molded to the growing curves of her breasts. The sight of her, followed by the unexpected hard jolt of desire, had turned his world upside down.

His guilt over his sudden lascivious turn of thoughts had set him on the road to destruction, prompted him to borrow Javier's Bugatti and take the curves of the winding mountain roads too fast on the way to a party he had initially turned down an invite to.

With his other best friend in the passenger seat. A friend who hadn't even wanted to get out that night.

"I grew up, Anna. It happens to most of us."

Her shoulders tensed. He swore again. Why was he so on edge with her? What had happened to him, to William, wasn't her fault. A large part of his goal in offering this arrangement had been to rectify the hurt he'd caused her, not add to it.

"Perhaps you're right."

Her soft voice reminded him of a day he'd discovered her talking with her uncle, Diego, who still served the Cabrera family as the butler at their Granada estate. She'd spoken quietly, almost meekly. Usually, when they'd spent time together, it had been just the two of them. He'd started to pay attention more after that, seen how Diego constantly warned her to be careful, set rules even stricter than Javier's guidelines for Alejandro.

The one person Diego had seemed to trust with Anna had been Antonio. Whether it was because he was the good child or because Isabella had initially encouraged the friendship, who could say. Back then, he'd taken the time Diego had given them and created as much fun as he could for the girl who, at first, had been a curiosity and a reprieve from loneliness. But over time, her sweetness, her growing confidence as she'd not only risen to but taken the reins on their adventures, her acceptance of him without expecting anything in return, had created a friend he hadn't been able to picture his life without.

And now he was decrying one of the things he'd loved most about spending time with her; her innocent joy.

An apology rose to his lips. His comment had

been out of line. He wanted to keep distance between them, yes, but not like this.

But before he could say sorry, she turned slightly and raised her chin. "Although I'd rather still believe in magic and fairy tales than become a stiff shirt who doesn't know how to have fun."

He stood frozen to the spot. No one talked to him like that. He took a few more steps until he was standing in front of her, an arm's reach away.

"Stiff shirt?"

She pinpointed him with gleaming eyes. "Shirt is the appropriate version of what first came to mind. I may be a dreamer, Antonio, but that doesn't make me stupid."

He ran a hand through his hair as he let out a frustrated sigh. "I never said you were stupid, Anna."

"You treating me like a child and making remarks like the one you just did implies enough. If you don't think that much of me, then why would you propose an idea that required spending time together?"

"I do like you," he ground out. "You were my best friend for years."

"Emphasis on 'were,'" she retorted. Where had this fire come from? Her spirit back then, strong as it was, had been energetic, bright, not this fierceness that blazed forth.

"We haven't been friends for some time, that's true." He stepped forward It was time to take charge of a situation that had spiraled wildly out of control. Another failure in his normally well-planned-out existence. "But we were friends. We can be again, or at least get along while we ride out this arrangement."

Ride was the wrong word to use. Because as he took another step closer, smelled the faintt scent of daisies, an image of Anna straddling his hips, her body rising up and down as she took him inside her, nearly knocked him off his feet.

"I don't know if I want to be friends with someone as priggish as you."

That stopped him short. "Adrian is priggish. I'm not."

She watched him for a long moment. With a huff, she started to swing her other leg up onto the railing. His heart jumped into his throat and he surged forward, one arm wrapping around her waist and snatching her back.

"Antonio!"

"That was foolish," he growled as he spun her away from the edge.

"How?" she cried as she placed both her hands on his chest to steady herself. "I was perfectly balanced, that railing is over a foot wide and there's a roof right below the railing."

"A roof that slants down and leads to a drop down a cliff side into the ocean," he snapped.

Fire snapped in her eyes. "You're just like my

tío. Controlling, overbearing, and suspicious of everyone."

The comparison ignited his anger. "So I'm like the man who kept you under lock and key? Me, the one who pulled you out of your grief and told you time and time again that you were capable of so much more than you gave yourself credit for?"

"That man is gone." Her chin tilted up. "The man I knew told me everything. The one in front of me is distant, bosses me around—" she leaned in "—and is hiding something."

Maldito. He started to pull back, but her fingers fisted in his shirt, refusing to let him go. The electricity charging through the night air crackled, changed from angry to sensual in the span of a heartbeat. Her beautiful gaze widened, her eyes drifting down to his lips then back up, searching for answers he didn't have.

Her fingers fisted in his shirt, the slight scrape of her nails through the fabric making him suppress a groan of need. He needed to let go of her, needed to put distance between them.

"Antonio…"

Her voice nearly undid him. Husky, filled with naked desire. When she'd confessed her feelings on the slopes of the mountains where they'd spent so many hours running wild, it had been shyly, sweetly. Now her voice filled him, electrified every vein. His hands tightened on her waist as his gaze fell on her lips, slightly parted, ready to be kissed...

No!

He stepped back so quickly she stumbled forward. He caught her arm and, once she was steady, released her as if she'd turned to molten lava and walked away.

Away from desire. Away from temptation. It had been so much easier to keep his distance when he'd known he would devastate her world again if he hurt her.

Except it wouldn't crush her. She'd be hurt, but she would do what she had after the magazine article—rise from the ashes and move on. It wasn't just about sex, either. It would have been so much easier if it was just physical. No, *she* interested him. Anna and her courageous leap from the suffocating love of her family and being unemployed to living in Paris, pursuing her dreams, walking a catwalk and making changes instead of excuses when she realized what she could do better in her own work.

Unlike him. As he stalked out the front door of his suite and down the hall to the elevator, the past roared in with a vengeance, the screech of rubber on asphalt mixing with William's shout of fear before the world went dark.

He punched the button for the first floor, his hands trembling with suppressed self-rage and grief and guilt.

He didn't deserve happiness. No amount of atonement would ever make him worthy of happiness, let alone being with someone like Anna Vega.

CHAPTER ELEVEN

ANNA STARED AT her reflection in the full-length mirror. She'd pulled her hair into a loose bun at the base of her neck. A video chat with Kess had confirmed that her sundress, a creamy creation with pale green ivy tangling over the bodice and full skirt paired with a wide-brimmed straw hat, was a solid choice for "lunch on the terrace" in Positano. When she'd first spied this material, she'd thought of a gown inspired by the forest surrounding Sleeping Beauty's castle. The dress had morphed after Paris into a summery concoction with ties on the shoulders for a vintage vibe and an open back for a hint of sexiness. Not the kind of look that would have worked for Kess's show, but perfect for her first outing.

Pride had her raising her chin. Like the gold gown, this dress felt *right*. Hopefully, it would capture the right attention when she and Antonio went out for lunch.

Her mind strayed for the fiftieth time to the disaster of last night. When he'd pulled her tight against his body, irritation had fled, replaced by a desire so intense she'd nearly thrown caution to the wind and kissed him.

Embarrassment had been her first reaction, followed swiftly by confusion and a hint of anger. The man made no sense. In Rome, he'd been polite but aloof. That is, until the Via Margutta, when she'd caught glimpses of her old friend. Now... now he vacillated between an overly protective big brother and a cold, distant ass who kept secrets very close to his well-toned muscular chest. She'd told him she didn't know who he was anymore. Judging by his ever-changing demeanor, he didn't, either.

After he'd left, she'd curled up in one of the chairs with her book and tried over and over to read. But after an hour of gazing blankly at the same page, she'd finally gone into his luxurious suite, crawled beneath the silk sheets and fallen asleep...only to wake every hour to see if he'd returned. When she'd finally awoken to sun streaming in through the stunning floor-to-ceiling windows, it had been to a empty penthouse suite.

A knock on the door echoed off the walls and made her jump.

"Ready?"

Antonio's deep voice vibrated through the door. She inhaled deeply. She could do this.

She crossed the suite, her sandals noiseless on the plush Turkish rug. The door swung open silently, giving her a moment to gaze at Antonio standing in the hallway. Dressed in khaki slacks, a perfectly tailored black polo and a stainless-steel watch that probably cost more than her first car, he looked every inch the suave billionaire. Handsome, controlled, with a slight edge to his stance that told everyone who looked upon him that *he* was in charge.

Yet as her eyes drifted up to his face, to the slight curve up of his lips and the softness around his eyes as he looked down at his phone, her heart twisted. She still saw her friend hidden behind the walls he'd constructed over the years. What had happened to make him so buttoned up and reserved?

Don't go there. Business arrangement, not a happy reunion. Be strong.

With that reminder echoing in her head, she walked into the hall. Antonio glanced up.

"One of yours?"

"Yes."

The smile that spread over his face melted her insides.

So much for staying strong.

"Those bastards don't know what they're missing."

The statement made her laugh. "What?"

He walked forward and, before she could steel herself, grabbed a hand and twirled her in a circle. The skirt flared out in a billowing cloud. As she spun around, she caught sight of Antonio's infectious grin, the crinkles at the corners of his eyes, glowing golden brown in the sunlight streaming in from the balcony. A moment that was exceptionally dangerous, chipping away at her defenses and letting wispy tendrils of emotions long buried through.

But, she told herself as she stopped spinning and the skirt settled against her legs with a delicious silky softness, a moment she would always remember. One of those that, on bad days, she would summon and relive over and over.

"It's an incredible dress."

"Thank you. It's one of my favorites," she added shyly.

The smile disappeared from his face as quickly as it had appeared, leaving her unsteady on her feet, as if she'd just been hit by a rogue wave on the beach. She'd thought he was sweeping last night's disaster under the rug. But apparently not. Regret flickered through her. She stood behind everything she'd said, except for comparing him to her uncle. As irritating as his protectiveness had been, she'd overreacted. There was a big difference between her uncle installing a tracking app on her phone and Antonio not wanting her to fall off a balcony.

"Let's go."

He walked to the door and opened it for her. A gentlemanly gesture, but he barely looked at her as she walked into the hallway. On their ride down in the elevator, he stood on the opposite side, eyes fixed on the numbers as they descended.

Well, this is going great. How were they supposed to sell a fake relationship when he could barely handle being in the same elevator?

The number dinged to floor two. She readied herself to walk out into the lobby alone.

Until warm fingers threaded through her own. Her gasp bounced off the mirrored walls, her cheeks growing hot. A glance at the mirror showed no reaction from Antonio, just that same intense gaze on the numbers. Maybe he'd been so lost in his own thoughts he hadn't heard her. Although, how he wasn't affected by their palms pressed together was beyond her.

Because you're Anna. Little Anna Vega and he's never wanted you.

Harsh talk from her rational brain, but it threw a much needed dose of cold water on her out-of-control hormones. The elevator stopped, the doors swooshed open, and she walked into the lobby with a poise she didn't feel.

Antonio called out a greeting to a group of workers standing off to the side clustered around blueprints, hailing several by name. At least he hadn't lost his appreciation for his employees. He'd always treated the staff at the mansion like they were people versus minions there to do his bidding.

She smiled at the men and they smiled back, one even giving her a playful wink. Antonio's hand tightened around hers and he tugged her forward toward the double doors. The limo sat in all its gleaming luxurious glory right outside.

"Do you always take the limo?" she asked as a chauffeur walked around to open the door.

"Yes."

She frowned as he sat across from her. "Why?"

"I don't drive."

He bit out the words so tersely that she refrained from asking any more questions and instead focused on the passing scenery outside her window.

Ten minutes later, Antonio escorted her down a lane filled with boutiques and storefronts, each one overflowing with flowers, jewelry and other handmade goods. As they walked past a clothing stall, a flash of color caught her eye.

"Oh!"

Her feet moved of their own accord, drawn as if the material called her name in a language only she could hear. A bolt of deep, seductive, red silk partially unraveled over a table. The threads sparkled, the specks of silver set into the scarlet fabric glinting like far-off stars. She reached out and the material flowed over her hand like water.

"Buongiorno."

Anna looked up to see a tall man with a kind smile set into a weathered, craggy face. He nodded at the silk.

"Beautiful, no?"

"It's stunning," she breathed.

"Handwoven by myself and my wife." He pointed to the barely visible threading along the edge. "Handwoven silk blends in with the color compared to machine-woven." He took up the other end of the material and rubbed it between his wrinkled fingers. The soft crunch made Anna smile.

"Like snow underfoot."

"Exactly, *signorina*." His smile widened in pride. "One of the marks of true silk."

"How much?"

He named a price that made her inwardly wince. It was more than a fair price for handwoven Italian silk. Back in Florence, she'd most likely pay twice that at one of the luxury stores dotting the city. But with so much of her budget already consumed by her rent in Paris and her living expenses, she couldn't afford the splurge right now.

"Perhaps my next visit."

She looked up and realized Antonio had disappeared. Had she upset him? She'd broken off without a word. Rude, but not intentionally so. She glanced around the crowded lane.

There.

It was like watching a sea part as Antonio walked toward her, his eyes concealed by sunglasses. People stood to the side, watching him out of the corners of their eyes or, in the case of one bold woman, with open admiration.

He stopped in front of her, a small violet gift bag hanging from his fingers.

"I wondered where you were," she said, her voice coming out breathier than she'd intended.

Before she could blink, he leaned down and pressed a quick kiss to her lips. The light caress sent electric currents charging through her arms, her legs, everywhere. Her eyes fluttered shut. She was about to stand on her tiptoes to return the kiss when she felt him step back.

"For you, *mariposa*."

Butterfly. He'd called her that the first time he'd taken her out into the wilderness beyond the walls of the Cabrera family estate. He'd laughed and called her *mariposa* because she "flitted from flower to flower." And she had, soaking up the first bit of joy she'd found since her parents had been taken from her as she'd rambled over the grassy slopes. Between the nights she'd awaken crying for her mom to the tears that had formed in Tío Diego's eyes the first few weeks anytime he'd seen her, tears that had made her agree to his laundry list of stringent conditions, Antonio's invitation to get out of the house had been a life-saver she'd desperately needed.

It felt like butterflies were fluttering in her stomach as she accepted the gift bag and opened it. Inside, wrapped in lavender tissue paper, was a diamond tennis bracelet.

"Oh!"

Not cubic zirconia. Not paste gems. No, these were real diamonds, a row of them set in silver with a hidden clasp. Antonio lifted it from the tissue paper and wrapped the diamonds around her wrist, his fingertips skimming the underside of her arm. A place, she learned as she froze, that was incredibly sensitive as he secured the clasp.

She looked down at the bracelet and nearly gulped. How much had it cost? Ten thousand? Fifteen? More? She was probably wearing nearly a year's worth of rent for her Paris apartment on her arm.

"You didn't have to do that, you know."

"I know. But I wanted to."

The simple statement warmed her. Even though it wasn't the kind of bracelet she would normally wear, the thought had been very kind. She started to reply, to echo her thanks once more, but he continued.

"There was a photographer just behind us. Between yesterday and today, we should be giving them plenty to talk about."

The bracelet grew heavy around her wrist, no longer a stunning piece of jewelry but a manacle. Of course the gift had been for show. So had the kiss.

So much for staying removed. Less than twenty-four hours from making her commitment to maintain a professional attitude toward this arrangement and she was already entertaining thoughts that any action Antonio took even hinted at his harboring feelings for her.

Self-pity beckoned. But the strength she'd slowly been building ever since her job loss surged forward, rescuing her from that precarious cliff. After this whole arrangement was over, she'd give the bracelet back.

She raised her chin. She didn't need Antonio to find her attractive to be happy. Emboldened, she leaned her head against his shoulder. "If not, perhaps this will." She leaned up and kissed his bearded cheek. When he looked down at her, she smiled, her reflection mirrored in his glasses. "Can't have you doing all the work."

CHAPTER TWELVE

OVER THE NEXT few days, Antonio and Anna fell into a routine. They spent their mornings apart, Anna on the balcony and Antonio holed up in his office. Just before noon, Antonio would collect her and they'd go out to lunch at one of the many restaurants.

What he'd planned as a subtle way to be seen had turned into exquisite torture. Anna wasn't like the women he'd dated over the last few years. Instead of pushing salad around her plate with a fork or turning her nose up at a slightly charred quiche crust, she enjoyed her food. The way her eyes lit when the waiter had placed a plate of caprese salad in front of her, the little moan of pleasure when she'd savored a forkful of pasta pomodoro...

That moan tortured him. She wasn't immune to him. He caught the subtle glances, the flush in her cheeks. Yet her response seemed to be purely physical. She played the role of girlfriend when they were out and about. In private, though, she remained as aloof as he did, disappearing onto the balcony all morning and all evening once they returned from their afternoon activity. The first day, after he'd gifted her the bracelet and they'd enjoyed lunch on the terrace at an exclusive bistro, he'd been relieved that she had put so much distance between them.

But the second day, as they'd wandered through one of Positano's many art galleries and she'd grabbed his arm, dragging him over to an oil painting of a beach, he'd felt...happy. Happier than he had been in a long time. New emails dinging his inbox every minute, contracts to review for Le Porto, and he couldn't have cared less. He'd basked in Anna's enthusiastic joy over a painting that cost a fraction of the bracelet he'd bought her, soaking up her sunshine like a man who'd been jailed for ages in the darkest dungeon. The third day, Anna had sweet-talked him into pizza and red wine over the fancy hilltop restaurant he'd picked out. Whether it was her luminous eyes as she bit into a slice topped with cheese and fresh basil or her sigh of contentment as she'd sipped her wine, he'd felt his own tension bleed out of his shoulders.

At night, the guilt that lurked all day beneath the blissful distractions Anna offered translated into nightmares the likes of which he hadn't experienced since right after the accident. He knew what his terrors were telling him; that he didn't deserve any of this. That he was gleaning too much joy from these sojourns with Anna.

God help him, he couldn't stop. Even the suffering of waking up to the memory of William's gaping mouth, blood trickling from his lips as he'd gasped like a fish and clawed at Antonio's arm, was worth the pleasure of her company, the moments of happiness he hadn't experienced in over a decade.

The news had been humming, churning out steady pictures of his and Anna's adventures around Positano. His tactic of basing their fake relationship out of his newest hotel had also worked, with a significant uptick in both media attention and reservation inquiries.

Except those indicators of success had fallen flat in the face of the enjoyment he was getting out of being around his old friend. His old friend who had the most stunning legs, a thousand-watt smile and a zest for life's simplest pleasures.

An intoxicating mix. One that was pulling him ever deeper into the quagmire he'd tried to avoid ten years ago. Because the more time he spent in Anna's company, the more he wanted her. Case in point: when he'd spied her bare wrist as she'd walked out onto the balcony a couple of days ago, his chest had tightened. He liked seeing the bracelet on her wrist.

He'd paid more attention and realized that she only wore the bracelet when they went out. She clasped it on her wrist just before they walked out of the penthouse and removed it almost as soon as the door clicked shut. At first it had irritated him. Now it grated. A fifteen-thousand-dollar diamond bracelet.

Yes, he grudgingly admitted to himself, it wasn't the kind of gift Anna would normally have liked. He'd seen her drawn to the silk, the way she'd lovingly caressed it. The sight of her fingers trailing so seductively over the material had made him turn away in time and spied the jewelry store and the photographer almost simultaneously. It had seemed like a perfect opportunity. Yet every time he'd seen her take the bracelet off, her movements had been jerky, almost frantic.

He'd bought jewelry for previous lovers, even diamonds, so long as they didn't land on anyone's finger. It was expected. Even though Anna was nothing like his former paramours, they had at least enjoyed his gifts.

What was wrong with it? And, more annoyingly, why did it bother him so much?

He walked into the penthouse forty-five minutes early. A shower, a change of clothes and then he would whisk Anna off to Santa Maria Church. Given how she'd reacted to a simple painting, he could only imagine her face when she saw the white and gold interior of the twelfth-century chapel.

What the hell are you doing?

He stopped cold in the middle of the living room. When had his plans become about Anna, about enjoying his time with her? When had his focus shifted?

Now was not the time to surrender his control.

He ran a hand through his hair. This was what happened when one rushed into a situation without proper analysis. When one made decisions based on emotions. The last time he'd done that, desperate to take a risk and do something for a thrill, he'd coerced William into doing something he hadn't wanted, something that had nearly gotten him killed.

He'd written to William after the accident, a letter full of apologies and offers to do whatever it took to give his former friend anything he desired. William had written back, told Antonio he didn't blame him for what had happened. But the references to how well physical therapy was going, that the doctors had been hopeful about his walking again, had been stakes in Antonio's heart, driving home the irrefutable fact that he'd hurt someone he cared about because of his own selfishness.

Pushing Anna away, not taking advantage of the incredible gift she'd offered him, had been one of the most selfless things he'd done.

If he didn't get this whirlwind of emotions for Anna under control, his rejection of her all those years ago would be a waste. Not to mention their plan, which they were now committed to with all of the press coverage, could blow up in both their faces.

A frown crossed his face. Between monitoring the press, overseeing the final phases of construction and enjoying his afternoons with Anna, he hadn't even asked about whether news of their supposed relationship had elicited any results for her designs.

Self-absorbed bastard.

Guilt, his most frequent companion, seeped into his skin. Reluctantly, he let his feet guide him to the balcony doors and stepped outside.

And stopped, his mouth dropping open.

The immediate surface looked just as it had, with two white lounge chairs arranged to look out over the balcony railing at the sea beyond, a matching table between to hold drinks, a book, whatever the sittees desired. For him, usually a laptop or business reports.

The balcony ran another thirty feet past the doors, with soaring columns and a netted ceiling covered in bougainvillea and ivy. Fans whirred silently, capturing the salty air drifting up off the waves and dispersing it in a gentle breeze over the artfully-arranged plush chairs and fire pit. At the far end, a wooden dining table had been arranged with ten chairs for the exceptionally rare occasion when Antonio would host private guests for dinner.

The table had been taken over by fabrics of all

colors and styles. A thin rope had been strung between two columns, papers hanging by clothespins. In the midst of the mess, sitting on the stone floor with headphones over her ears, was Anna.

Oblivious to his presence, her hand flew over the paper, a pencil clutched in her hand. That thick, dark hair his fingers itched to touch had been pulled up into a ponytail. His gaze moved over her like he hadn't seen her in years, from her pert nose and defined cheekbones to her full lips and dark lashes hiding her eyes. His stare drifted down to the form-fitting black tank and lime-green running shorts.

Desire crashed into another emotion; a craving he couldn't quite describe. The bucolic scene before him stirred a longing in him, a longing not just to sweep the fabric off the table and lay Anna down beneath him, but to sit beside her on the floor, ask questions about her designs, watch her sparkle as she shared her passion with him.

Danger!

Retreating had never been a part of his DNA, not since he'd gone off to college. But if he didn't now, he risked one of two things: kissing the daylights out of Anna Vega or crossing the line into emotional territory that would be hell to crawl out of.

He took a step back, ready to turn. A gull soared between the columns, landed on the fire pit and uttered a loud, attention-seeking squawk.

Anna looked up, smiling at the bird, before her gaze landed on him. Her mouth formed a little *O* as her eyes widened. The bird, damn him, glanced between the two with a rapid jerk of its head, turned and flew off.

Leaving Anna and Antonio alone on the balcony.

How long had Antonio been out there? Anna slowly removed her headphones, her heartbeat kicking into high gear. The pounding in her ears competed with the roar of the surf below.

"Um…hi."

"Hello."

Why did the man have to look so…calm? So in control? Eleven in the morning and he looked like he'd just walked off an Armani photo shoot in black pants that caressed his muscular thighs and a hunter-green polo fitted perfectly to his shoulders. His dark hair had been swept back from his face, probably to taunt her with those chiseled cheekbones and sinful brown eyes. Even his stubble looked sexy yet contained, shaved in a perfect line that drew attention to the defined cut of his jaw.

Except…her eyes drifted down and landed on his bare feet. Maybe it was the sight of bare skin. Maybe it was the glimpse of something vulnerable in the otherwise stalwart Antonio Cabrera. Whatever it was, it sparked something inside her.

Her head jerked back up to meet his neutral gaze. "Were we going out early today?"

"No. I came up to shower and wandered out here." He nodded behind her. "I didn't realize you had set up office."

She winced. "Sorry. I should have asked." She waved a hand toward the palatial suite. "I didn't feel comfortable taking over your space."

He cocked his head to one side. "Despite your newfound confidence, you say 'sorry' a lot. Did you always apologize this much?"

"When?"

"Before."

So much in that one word. Before they'd grown up. Before she'd gone and fallen in love, or at least developed a crush that had felt like love in her teenage mind. Before he'd broken her heart with cruel words she'd never expected to hear from the lips of the one person she'd thought understood her better than anyone.

"I did to others. My aunt and uncle especially."

"But not me."

"No," she agreed softly. "Not you."

With her aunt and uncle, she'd apologized whenever she had frightened them, which had been often. Eight minutes late getting home from school? Apology. Traipsed out of phone range in the vineyards and hadn't returned a text? Apology. Decided to move out of her childhood bedroom and go to Paris at the age of twenty-seven? Apology.

Kess had wanted to ride into battle for her, tell her aunt and uncle how much they'd scarred her with their incessant worrying. Anna had always stopped her. Not only did she love her aunt and uncle, but deep down she knew the fears that had driven their helicopter parenting style. She'd felt the same fears whenever they'd gone into Granada for a date night, had waited at the top of the stairs with her phone clutched in her hands, every *ping* sending fear spiraling through her veins. It hadn't been until she'd seen the headlights illuminating the driveway that she'd heaved a sigh of relief and crept off to bed.

Perhaps it had been the lifeline of distraction Antonio had first offered. How he'd been one of the few not to incessantly ask how she was doing. How he hadn't been afraid to tease her, to push her to do things on her own, to treat her like she was just another kid instead of an *orphan*.

So many reasons why they'd become friends. So many reasons why she'd fallen for him.

But that boy had disappeared. Whatever had happened that last week in Granada before he'd gone back to university had hardened him. Every time she slipped on that bracelet, the cool metal on her wrist served as a reminder that their relationship was an act.

Yet the last few days had been different. He'd

seemed relaxed, happier. It had been all too easy to enjoy spending time with him instead of keeping her guard up.

"Is this just for fun?" He gestured to the drawings behind her and the swaths of fabric she'd picked up at a boutique.

"No." Shyness crept in. She tapped out a nervous rhythm with the pencil against the paper in her hand. "I actually got a call. Well, a couple."

There it was again, that damned genuine smile that blazed across his face and turned his eyes from opaque brown to sinful chocolate.

"That's great."

Add the warmth in his tone to those devastating eyes and she could feel her bones turning to mush as she ducked her face to hide the blush his praise brought on.

"Thanks."

His bare feet whispered across the stone as he walked over to her and crouched down. He reached out again, like he had in Rome, and tilted her chin up. In Rome, it had been electric, that touch of his skin on hers. Here, with questions swirling in her mind and emotions battling in her chest, she wanted nothing more than to lean into his touch and soak in his strength.

Weak.

She pulled back, ignoring the flash in his eyes. No way was Antonio Cabrera hurt. She was seeing things she wanted to see.

"Why are the calls not good news?" His voice came out terse.

"They are."

"But?"

She sighed and sat back, pulling her legs into her chest.

"One was from a contest that had previously said they were full. Suddenly, they magically have an opening to consider my work. Two labels called, asking for a sample portfolio."

"Good labels?"

"Very good. Like never-in-a-million-years good. But," she continued as he opened his mouth to prompt her once more, "I submitted to them in May and they turned me down."

"Which means our plan is working."

She rested her forehead on her knees. "It does. It just…" She sucked in a breath. "What if it's only because of our fake relationship? What if this has nothing whatsoever to do with my talent?"

She was being torn in so many different directions. Ecstatic that her designs were finally getting a chance. Guilty that it most likely had little to do with her actual work and everything to do with her fake relationship with a famous billionaire.

And beneath it all, that pulse of awareness that jolted through her veins every time she and Antonio stepped out into the public eye. If she didn't have the reminder of the bracelet on her wrist, he could have convinced her that he felt something more than commitment to their charade.

Hands wrapped around her biceps.

Her head snapped up as Antonio hauled her to her feet and spun her around, keeping his hands cupped on her shoulders. Shock and the lightning that zapped from his hands across her skin kept her mute, allowing him to move her around like a rag doll.

"Do you see what I see?"

She blinked at the drawings in front of her. Some of them were good. Some of them were very good. All of them were *hers*. Instead of replicating, she'd opened the floodgates on her creativity and drawn what she'd felt instead of playing it safe. These designs had elements of royalty, the kind of touches that would make any woman feel like a princess. But the creations were all hers.

"Um…drawings?"

"Damned good ones."

His cursing teased a smile from her.

"Thank you. But how do you know these are good? What do you know about women's fashion?"

"I know enough."

Those three words dropped with icy cold precision into the pit of her stomach. Of course he knew. He dated supermodels and women with their own business empires. Fashion. Textile fabrication. Media.

"True." She wrenched that word out and started to pull away.

Antonio turned her around. "Why do you do this to yourself?"

"Do what?"

"Convince yourself you're not good enough? Talk yourself down?" He sounded angry.

She wanted to throw her hands up and scream. Yes, she was scared she wasn't good enough. But scared didn't translate to the end of the world. Not anymore. Just because she was scared didn't mean she would stop designing, stop trying. If she needed any evidence that he didn't see the new her, the woman who stumbled and fell but picked herself back up—figuratively and literally—then he would never see her.

"Go."

She managed to force the word out. She was done with people coddling her, ignoring the progress she'd made, the things she'd accomplished. All they saw was failure, meekness, innocence. Why could none of them see that even her failures were successes, stepping stones to helping her become not just a designer but a stronger woman, a better person?

Silence reigned. He'd let go of her shoulders but she knew he hadn't left, could still smell his woodsy cologne, feel the electric charge between their bodies.

At last, she looked up. Antonio stared at her,

the blank expression back. Here she was, an emotional mess on the verge of letting tears of frustration flow, and he looked at her like she could have been a former friend on the verge of a meltdown or a stack of reports that required his attention. Both equally irritating, a nuisance in his otherwise structured life.

She started to walk past him. His arm shot out. She tried to duck under, but he lowered his arm and looped it around her waist, hauling her back against his chest. She turned, prepared to tell him to leave, to give her the day to get her head back in the game.

Except her hands landed on his chest, his muscles hard beneath her touch. His heart pulsed beneath her fingers, fast and furious. The warmth of his skin penetrated through his shirt. It wound through her veins, making her light-headed as she sucked in a breath. Her chest filled with the scent of *him*.

Dazed, she looked up. His eyes captured hers. They weren't just molten chocolate. No, they were a blazing mahogany brown. Her lips parted. He wanted her. Desired her. She wasn't just imagining it.

His gaze drifted to her mouth at the same time his hips pressed against hers. She gasped at the sensation of his hardness pressed against her thighs, arched into him as an ache built deep inside her.

"Antonio…"

A growl emanated from his chest. And then he leaned down and kissed her.

Danger!

Antonio had sailed clear past danger and was firmly in *Oh, hell* territory. But he couldn't have stopped if he'd wanted to.

Which he most definitely didn't want to. Anna fit perfectly in his arms, her slim body pressed against him as if she couldn't bear to leave even a sliver of daylight between them. Even though his lust demanded that he claim her, he kissed her slowly, caressing her lips with his own, cradling her head in one hand while he kept the other firmly pressed against her back.

If she pulled back, he'd let her go. But, dear God, he hoped she wouldn't. He would regret this later.

Later. Not now when she felt so good in his arms. So *right*.

And then she came alive. She moaned, throwing her arms around his neck. His fingers grasped at the ponytail band, pulling it out of her hair and tangling in the long locks that tumbled down her back.

Somewhere in the far recesses of his rational mind was the fact that he was kissing not only his former best friend, but his former *virginal* best friend.

It should have stopped him. But when he started to pull away, Anna simply pressed that incredible body against his. With a groan, he reached down, grabbed her thighs and hoisted her up in the air, spinning her around to set her on the table. She gasped into his mouth and he dove in, his tongue slipping in to taste her. The intimacy of the moment made him so hard he could barely stand it.

And Anna, his sweet, innocent Anna, kissed him right back. Her hands tugged at his shirt, pulled it free from the waistband of his pants. Her fingers grazed the tip of his erection straining past his belt. He reared back.

Anna stared at him, eyes wide and luminous. "I... I..."

Before she could apologize, he swooped in again, crushing her body against his as he kissed her once more. Her legs spread as she inched her bottom closer to the edge of the table and pressed her core against his hardness.

"Oh, God, yes."

Her fevered words pushed him on, her hands creeping under his shirt and splaying across his rib cage. He reached down, ready to rip off his shirt, then hers, feel her bare breasts against his skin.

He wrenched his mouth from hers, started to trail searing kisses over her cheek, down her neck.

"Yes, Antonio!"

His name cut through the madness that had

seized him. Hearing her say his name as she had a thousand times before sent a series of memories careening through his mind. Anna, in her black skirt and shirt, looking so lost in the palatial opulence of his parents' home. Anna, waiting for him by his locker after class. Anna, in her virginal white, telling him how much she loved him.

You are not worthy.

He yanked away from her so quickly he nearly stumbled.

"Anna…" He ran a hand through his hair, his breath coming in short gasps as he tried to get his raging lust under control. Hard to do when Anna sat right in front of him, legs splayed, breasts heaving as she sucked in deep breaths, lips swollen, hair tumbling past her shoulders in a sexy, rumpled mess.

It almost undid him. Almost. She wanted him. He wanted her. They were two consenting adults, no longer a young man raging with hormones and a teenager who didn't know any better.

But Anna deserved better than a quick lay. She deserved forever. And he deserved nothing she had to offer.

For the second time that week, and the third time in his life, Antonio walked away from Anna Vega.

CHAPTER THIRTEEN

ANNA'S ARMS SLUICED through the warm waters of the Tyrrhenian Sea as she made her tenth lap across the cove. It had been ages since she'd indulged in a swim. With so much energy zipping through her veins, the sight of the long stone staircase winding down to the private beach she'd discovered as she'd explored the hotel had been too enticing to pass up.

Plus, it got her outside. Even though she hadn't seen Antonio at all since he'd walked away yesterday, she knew he was still inside. When she'd finally summoned up the courage to go downstairs and seek out something to eat, she'd smelled a wisp of his cologne in the elevator. Paul had arched a skeptical brow when she'd asked to go into town alone, but he'd done it. She'd waited by the empty flower beds, staring at the smooth earth, when she'd felt a hot flicker of awareness between her shoulder blades. But when she'd turned and raked her eyes over the windows of the front of the hotel, they'd been empty.

The afternoon had passed in a whirlwind. Relaxing beneath the red-striped umbrellas on Marina Grande Beach after a dip in the water. Sipping on a glass of Aperol Spritz on the patio of Franco's, an upscale bar overlooking the ocean. Savoring lemon sorbet from a street vendor.

None of it helped. The sea, the drink, the dessert. None of it cooled the banked coals of lust Antonio had ignited with his incredible kiss.

It also didn't soothe the tension that had gripped her ever since she'd seen the sorrow in his eyes as he'd pulled away. The last few days, seeing how relaxed he'd been, echoes of who he used to be swirled in with the confident leader he'd become, had tugged at loose heartstrings. She saw how he interacted with Paul and the construction workers, the respect he gave those who worked for him. And the way he planned their sojourns, remembering little things she liked from long ago like no walnuts on her salad and a preference for as little ice as possible in her drinks, had made her feel known, an intimacy almost deeper than the soul-searing kiss they'd shared.

Why had he pulled away? What demons was he fleeing?

A rogue wave snuck up and smacked her in the face. She sucked in a gulp of salt water and coughed. The salt stung her throat as she came upright, trying to keep her head above water as her feet flailed for purchase.

An arm encircled her waist and pulled her into shallower waters. Her feet hit the sand and she bent over, coughing and trying to push her hair out of her eyes.

"You're okay, just breathe."

Antonio's voice broke through the pain of the salt water still stinging her throat. She scraped her wet hair back to see him staring at her, eyes wide, nostrils flared.

"What do you—" Her question was cut off by another round of coughing.

Before she could finish, Antonio scooped her up in his arms and carried her out of the sea to where she'd set her towel and beach bag. As her coughing abated, she pushed against his chest and tried to swing her legs out of his grasp. She might as well have been pushing against a mountain for all the good it did her.

With the coughing fit over and the pain receding, the sensation of being cradled in Antonio's strong embrace hit her with the force of a freight train. Paul had confirmed that the beach was private and would only be available to Le Porto's guests. The only way in and out was the stone staircase. So she'd pulled on an emerald bikini she'd picked up when shopping with Kess in Rome, the tie-string bottom and halter top showcasing way more skin than the one pieces she normally favored. Now, with so little on, she could feel every inch of his bare arms on her skin, his fingertips pressed firmly on her thigh.

The memory of how brazenly she'd pressed herself against him yesterday made her blush. What had come over her? She might be a virgin, but she'd certainly been kissed before. Never, though, had any of the boys she'd kissed, or been kissed by, in college ever come close to eliciting that kind of aching desire in her.

Antonio knelt next to her towel and set her down as if she were made of spun glass, his face turning from concerned to thunderous even though his movements remained tender.

"Are you all right?"

She nodded, keeping her eyes on the horizon. Why was he down here? Had he come to apologize? Or finish what they'd started on the balcony?

"Yes, I'm fine. I just swallowed a little water." Finally, she turned to look at him.

And promptly wished she hadn't.

He'd worn khaki shorts and a black T-shirt for his trip down to see her. After going into the water to rescue her, his shirt was molded to his powerful frame, outlining every muscle beneath. She'd felt those muscles yesterday when she'd ripped his shirt out of his pants.

"Why were you swimming here alone? You should never swim by yourself."

The patronizing tone cut into her fantasy and

dragged her back to earth. Nothing had changed. Judging by his voice, yesterday had been an unusual occurrence, a brief moment when Antonio had seen her as a woman, not as a friend or child to be taken care of.

Short-lived.

Pre-Paris, that knowledge would have made her duck her head, apologize and scuttle off. But after the taste she'd just had of what physical pleasure could offer, of what she'd been teased with before having it yanked away, she found herself irritated.

"I spoke with Paul before I came down here. He said the cove had been vetted as a safe swimming spot and to just stay within the confines of the rocks."

Antonio ran a hand through his wet hair. "Still, you should have told someone where you were."

"I did," she replied testily. "Paul. I just told you that."

"I meant me."

"Why would I do that? You didn't care where I was yesterday after you had your fun." The anger in her voice surprised even her, but she didn't back down. Not this time. Yesterday she'd been so consumed by the revelations kissing Antonio had revealed, it had masked the confusion and years of thinking she hadn't been good enough, hadn't been desirable enough. It hadn't just been that Antonio had told her he didn't feel the same way. He'd *hurt* her.

He started to speak but she held up her hand. Strength and anger combined to create a confidence that surged through her and propelled her to her feet.

"One, I told Paul. I confirmed it was safe to swim here. Contrary to what you, my uncle and almost everyone else seems to think, I can make intelligent decisions."

"I never said—"

"No, but you implied it. Multiple times. And second, do you have any idea how confusing all of this is? Ten years ago you told me I was just a girl with her head in the clouds and that you would never want someone like me." He winced hearing his own words spoken aloud, pain flashing across his face, but she didn't let up. No, it was time for him to finally see how much he'd hurt her. "I thought something was wrong with me, that all my fears were true. The person I was when I was with you was just an illusion and one that you'd seen through." A sob rose in her throat, but she swallowed past it. She would *not* cry in front of him. "Your rejection was confirmation that I was fanciful, naïve. You told me I wasn't mature enough, wasn't good enough—"

"I remember every word I spoke that day," he ground out as he stood, "and I never said you weren't good enough."

The sob rose higher as her eyes grew hot. "It was implied."

He leaned forward and grabbed her by the shoulders. "No! I was the one who wasn't good enough. I will never be good enough for you."

The words hung in the air between them.

Antonio's chest rose and fell as he stared into her eyes, his expression deadly serious. She stared back, speechless.

"Anna, when you…when you told me how you felt…"

The pain in his voice wiped away her anger. She started to reach out, to lay a hand on his shoulder to comfort him, but stopped before she touched him.

"I had noticed you." She leaned forward, barely discerning his words over the waves splashing onto the beach and the gulls cawing overhead. "I'd noticed you the week before you told me how you felt."

"Noticed?"

His shoulders rose then fell as his breath came out in a *whoosh*.

"Physically."

Did the earth actually shift under her? Maybe it was watching the waves move up and down that gave her the sensation of being caught at sea, tossed back and forth in a maelstrom.

"So when you said you had no interest in me…"

"You're just a child, Anna."

The look of disgust on Antonio's face froze her in place as dread built in the pit of her stomach.

"We've had fun the last few years, but your head is always in the clouds. For God's sake, you're a child!" he repeated. "We could never be a couple."

She stared at him. "But... Antonio, I—"

"Don't say it." He cut her off. "I heard you the first time. You think you love me, Anna, but you don't. You love a fantasy you've built on fairy tales and who you think I am."

"That's not true!"

He laughed. A cruel, harsh sound that tumbled from his lips as he looked away from her toward the sun setting over Granada. Her heart ached as the golden light illuminated his face. How could he look so handsome when he was breaking her dreams into a thousand pieces?

Then his gaze swung back to her, pinned her in place as his brown eyes hardened. "It's best if whatever relationship we had ends now."

No! What had she done? If she'd just kept her mouth shut, if she hadn't told him how she felt, she'd still have her friend.

"Let's just pretend this never happened. I won't bring it up again, I promise."

He shook his head once.

"It's too late for that. Goodbye, Anna."

Antonio sucked in a shuddering breath. "I said what I had to. To get you to let go."

"So you made a decision for me?"

He turned to look at her, regret hanging over

him in a heavy cloud that enshrouded her in his
misery. Why had she accepted his words that day?
She'd known something was wrong. Antonio had
never spoken to her like that before, had never
treated her so cruelly. Yet she'd been so focused
on herself, on her own pain and humiliation, that
she'd let him walk away. If she'd been stronger
then, more confident like she was now, she would
have run after him, demanded answers.

Although as she stared at him, something else
tugged at her. He met her gaze head-on. Was it
the shifting of his feet, the slight twitch of his left
eye, or the subtle clenching of his fingers that told
her he wasn't being entirely truthful?

A tiny white scar above his left eyebrow caught
her attention, triggered a memory. When he'd dis-
missed her so coldly, the scar had been a wound,
ugly and red and barely visible beneath the tumble of dark hair that had fallen over his forehead.

Her hand came up, her fingers reaching out.
Antonio jerked back.

"Don't."

He bit the word out, as harsh as that horrible
day all those years ago. He turned to leave.

"You're really good at walking away, Cabrera."

He whirled around. The black T-shirt clung to
his body, the rippling of muscles beneath the wet
cloth reminding her of a panther. Sleek, fast, powerful.

"I don't deserve you, Anna." His voice, so gravelly, sent shockwaves of awareness rippling across her skin. She shivered. He swore and tugged her cover-up out of her bag, draping it over her shoulders and tugging it over her almost-nude body. "I'm not interested in marriage. Never have been, doubt I ever will be. It wasn't on my radar to begin with, and after what I've seen, I don't want it." A hoarse laugh escaped him. "My mother is under a delusion that she and my father were a love match, and I've never seen any evidence of that. You want what *your* parents had. Marriage and kids and the whole love-of-your-life bit. You told me so yourself."

She had. Numerous times. At first, they had been the ramblings of a teenage girl confiding in a friend. A longing for the kind of relationship her parents had had, one built on not just love but respect, admiration and friendship. What many would call a fairy tale.

Although, as far as she could remember, Prince Charming had never kissed his princess the way Antonio had kissed her yesterday, with a possessive fire that had seared her from head to toe.

"I never meant to put that kind of pressure on you, Antonio."

"I know. But what I felt for you…" His voice deepened. "It wasn't good. Not for someone like you. Not after what I did."

"What you did?" she repeated. "Antonio, talk to me."

The sorrow in his eyes nearly broke her. His hand came up and cupped her face.

She hadn't known true heartbreak before. In this moment, realizing that Antonio felt something for her, that he'd felt something for her back then and she'd been too cowardly to pursue him, to find out what had made her best friend act so terribly and that he was still carrying the weight of that secret all these years later, shattered her heart into a million pieces.

"I wish I could. Just know, Anna, what you made me feel back then..." A shuddering breath escaped him. "What I feel now..."

She swayed forward, hypnotized by the longing in his words.

"What do you feel?"

He stared at her for the longest time, so long she wondered if he'd heard her.

And then, finally.

"Hunger. Like I'm starving for you."

Antonio stepped out of an ice-cold shower and grabbed a towel, wrapping it around his hips. The water had done little to assuage his erection. Neither had his own touch, a few quick jerks meant to take the edge off.

Except when he'd touched himself, he'd imagined Anna's hands wrapped around him. When he'd found his release, he'd envisioned sliding into her body, hearing her gasp his name.

His fingers curled into fists as he stalked to the mirror. It had been a mistake to go searching for her, to apologize for the kiss. He never should have sought her out. He never should have confessed how he'd felt about her all those years ago. But when she'd stood up to him, her fire shadowing a deep-rooted hurt, and her gut-wrenching admission of how much his cruel words had affected the last ten years of her life, he hadn't been able to lie to her any longer.

Besides, it was better this way. Now she knew the truth, or at least most of it. He hadn't been able to bring himself to tell her about the accident. About William. About why he would always be alone.

He ran a comb through his hair, each stroke blunt and angry. Deep down, he was still the same reckless teenager who had nearly gotten his friend killed. Take last night. He'd given in to the slightest desire and had nearly taken Anna right then and there on the balcony table. Anna had proved time and again over the last week that she could take care of herself. That didn't mean she was impervious to the pain that would come from a man like him taking her virginity and then kicking her back into the real world. That he'd almost done just that was further evidence he wasn't, and never would be, the kind of man she deserved.

That was why, after he'd confessed how he'd actually felt all those years ago to Anna, he'd let his hand drop from her face before she could respond to his bold admission. He'd told her that if she no longer felt comfortable continuing their charade, he would arrange to have his helicopter fly her to Paris. She hadn't answered, had just nodded while staring out at the sea in that damned bikini that revealed the sensual swell of her breasts and legs he'd imagined wrapped around his waist last night.

Once more, he'd retreated. Each step up that long, winding staircase had killed him.

You've waited long enough. She wants you. What are you waiting for?

The need pulsed through him, insidious and hot. He pushed it away. If Anna decided to continue their charade through the wedding as they'd planned, he'd move into one of the guest suites. Paul could make up some excuse to the cleaning staff. Although it probably wouldn't be necessary. He'd revealed everything to her, and she'd barely been able to look at him when he'd left the beach.

Well, almost everything. When she'd asked him to talk to her, the story had risen and rested on the tip of his tongue. He'd wanted to tell her. Knowing that he would see only disgust in her eyes had stopped him.

God willing, the details of that night would never again see the light of day.

He stalked out of the bathroom, running through a mental checklist of what he would need to move into the suite down the hall should she stay. Computer, phone charger, toothbrush…

The scent of daisies hit him, stopped him in his tracks. He sucked in a shuddering breath then slowly, so slowly, raised his head to see Anna framed in the door leading out to the balcony, her slim form wrapped in a pale pink robe. Her hair tumbled down her back and over her shoulders in cascading waves of dark brown.

His mouth dried.

"Anna…what are you doing here?"

She stared at him for a long moment, as if trying to make up her mind about something. Then she stepped into the room.

"I want us to have sex."

His mind stuttered. His brain shouted *Danger!* even as his lust shouted back *Yes!*

"Perhaps you didn't hear me on the beach," he replied as coolly as he could manage.

She took another step. The sun hit the robe and illuminated her sensual figure through the thin material of her robe. His fingers curled on the doorway, a physical reminder to stay put.

"I won't be what you want, either."

Surprised, he asked, "How so?"

Her long lashes fluttered. "I do want it all. Eventually. Marriage, kids, love, flowers and romantic cards. You said yourself you'll never be that kind of man, and I'm not settling for less."

The words should have brought relief, not created an ache in his chest.

"That doesn't explain why you think we should have sex."

Was that his voice? The casual, almost bored, tone? How did he even achieve it when flames were licking over every inch of his skin?

His fingers dug deeper into the doorframe, so hard, he was surprised it didn't splinter beneath his grasp.

"You gave me a taste yesterday of something I'd never experienced before."

"A mistake that will not be repeated."

"What if I want you to repeat it?"

God, her voice. So breathless, so sweet and soft. How could he possibly give in to the temptation she was offering without hating himself for the rest of his life?

"You don't know what you're asking."

"But I do." Another step into the room. "I've kissed other men before."

Who? The possessive shout sounded from within, primal and jealous that any other man had laid a hand on her, much less his lips.

"And?"

This time his suave casualness had disappeared, the word coming out on a growl.

"And it was nothing like what I shared with you yesterday. I want more of that. You said yourself the world can be a bad place. What better way to be introduced to sex and the physical side of pleasure than with someone I know and trust?"

"You shouldn't trust me," he ground out. "I'm just going to break your heart."

"Only if I give it you," she countered. "I offered it to you once. I'm stronger now. Wiser. I won't make that mistake again."

Smart girl, even if that cut deep.

"But what I do want," she continued, "is to know more about sex."

He should say no, needed to say no.

Yet, his body argued, *she'll just find someone else to introduce her to sex. She knows where she stands with you. What if the man she finds breaks her heart or hurts her?*

Before his brain could come up with a logical counter, Anna reached up and parted the folds of the robe to reveal her body underneath.

Her nearly naked body.

CHAPTER FOURTEEN

Anna tweaked her shoulders and let the robe fall in a silken pool at her ankles. Amazing how she could stand in front of Antonio in just a bralette and thong without joining the robe on the floor. Outwardly, she tried to replicate what she'd seen when she'd spied the woman in the window in Rome. Confidence, poise, sensuality.

She hoped she was doing it right because inside she was a bundle of frayed nerves. Her heart slammed against her ribs. The bottom of her stomach had dropped and stayed somewhere down around her feet when Antonio had walked out of the bathroom, that towel casually wrapped around his waist, displaying his muscular abdomen, glistening wet from his shower.

Hearing what Antonio had had to say on the beach, realizing that he had lied to her all those years ago, that the desire he'd shown for her yesterday on the balcony had been real, had emboldened her. She had offered herself up once and failed to follow through when she'd known something had been wrong.

This time, she knew exactly how things stood. Antonio had made her feel things she'd never experienced with the few men she'd dated. If her career took off, there was no telling when she would find the time to meet someone, fall in love and get married. What better way to be introduced to the world of physical pleasure than by someone she knew? Someone she trusted? Even though he'd changed over the years, she found that she still trusted him. Even if he didn't trust her enough to share what had caused him to retreat into this closed-off persona.

And, if he rejected her, at least she could say she had tried this time.

The longer he stared at her, the more she steeled herself for his rejection. She'd handled it once and recovered. Armed with her newfound knowledge that he'd at least wanted her, it would hurt, but she would emerge from this.

He inhaled, the sound audible in the stillness that had settled over the room. His eyes moved from hers, sliding down her neck to her breasts, then further still over her stomach and down to the juncture of her thighs. The electricity in her veins hummed louder, sparking little fires throughout her body everywhere his gaze roamed.

Dear God, even if the man said no, at least

she would forever have this moment burned into her memory.

"Terms."

She blinked. "What?"

"I proposed our fake relationship with few terms and little forethought," he bit out. "What are the terms for this arrangement?"

A quiver raced through her. Was this actually happening? Was he saying yes?

"Um…well…" What was she supposed to ask for? She'd never had sex.

"Just the once?"

"I was thinking more throughout the remainder of our fake relationship."

One corner of his mouth twitched. "What if you don't like it?"

She snorted, her hand flying up a second later to cover her mouth in mortification. "Sorry. I just, uh, don't see that being a likely scenario."

His lips curved up more.

The heat in her core grew hotter. She shifted, suddenly acutely aware of the dampness on her thighs. Antonio's eyes flickered down to her legs, lingered, then slowly crawled back up her body.

"Protection."

"Of course," she agreed hurriedly.

"Anything else?"

She bit down on her lower lip. "I don't know. I've never done this before. Am I supposed to ask for a certain number of orgasms or something?"

He stared at her then threw his head back and laughed.

"God, Anna, you're going to be the death of me."

Before she could process that statement, he moved forward, his steps slow but sure. *Panther-like*, she thought again, as sunlight flowed over his muscles. Her eyes swung to where the towel clung to his hips. She'd seen superhero movies where the men had Vs carved into their stomachs that went down toward their thighs, a not so subtle trail to what lay between their legs. She never thought anyone actually looked like that.

But Antonio did, and he was coming straight for her like he was going to taste every inch of her body and make her go up in flames.

What have I done?

Then he was there, a breath away, the heat from his body seeping into hers. Her nipples hardened beneath the weight of his gaze. She kept her hands fixed at her sides. She would not touch herself, would not try to assuage the ache building so deep inside it almost hurt.

She expected to see the same raging lust in his eyes that she'd seen yesterday. But when their gazes collided, she saw desire mixed with a tenderness that tugged at the loose threads of the past.

"Are you sure?"

A pause. Then she nodded.

He slid his arms around her waist. This time

when she gasped, she didn't bother to hide her reaction. She embraced the arch of her body into his and savored the feel of her breasts pressing up against his chest. He leaned down and brushed his lips across hers, a whisper that made her whimper. She wanted the fire and passion of yesterday, the burning desire to touch each other everywhere.

But Antonio had other ideas. Every time she tried to deepen the kiss, tease him by stroking her fingers over his chest, nip his bottom lip, he simply smiled against her mouth and continued to kiss her as if she was the most precious treasure in the world.

Finally, she relaxed and let him explore, her body melting against his. His fingers skimmed up and down her back, leaving trails of tingling heat in their wake. She slowly eased her hands up the back of his neck and into his hair. Who knew touching someone's hair could be so erotic? When she tangled her fingers in the silky thickness, his kiss firmed, his tongue darting out and tracing the seam of her lips with masterful precision.

His hands moved with aching slowness over her waist, skimmed up her sides. A moan escaped her as he cupped her breasts. Her head lolled back. He left her mouth, pressed his lips to her cheek, then her jaw, then down her neck. He kissed her pulse beating frantically in her throat, his fingers working under the band of her bralette. Then he was pulling the lace up, over, and suddenly she was standing in front of him in nothing but her lace thong.

Her confidence wavered. She'd never been this close to being naked in front of a man before. It made her feel vulnerable.

Antonio must have sensed her hesitation because he paused, her bralette in one hand, the other fisted by his side.

"All you have to do is say 'stop,'" he whispered, "and I'll stop."

His reassurance soothed some of her uncertainty. It had nothing to do with him and everything to do with her own insecurities.

"I know." She reached up and laid her hand against his stubbled jaw. His gaze darkened and he turned, pressing a kiss to the middle of her palm that made her eyes drift shut. She'd never imagined the various parts of her body that could experience sensual pleasure. Each reveal elicited more joy, the physical delights mixing with her sense of adventure. If she'd known it could be like this, perhaps she would have sought out a partner sooner.

Although that wasn't true, she acknowledged as Antonio's hands returned to her bare breasts, cupping the globes in his hands. No one had ignited this need inside her. After Antonio's rejection, she hadn't trusted anyone else with her body. Ironic that the man who had broken her heart was also now touching her in ways she had only imagined.

He leaned down and captured a nipple in his mouth. She cried out, her hands returning to his hair as she pressed her breast more fully against him. His arms encircled her waist as he let out a primal growl that thrilled her to her toes. Each suck sent lightning arcing through her body. The hair on his jaw scraped across her breasts before his mouth latched onto her other nipple.

Before she could further explore his body, he scooped her up into his arms and carried her to the bed. He lowered her down as he had on the beach. Yet this time his lips fused to hers in another passionate kiss that made her toes curl and one hand grip the silky comforter while the other grabbed onto his shoulder. His muscles rippled beneath her touch, a steadiness she desperately needed as her emotions rose and fell like the waves on the beach. Excitement, elation, desire, need…beneath it all, running so deep she almost missed it in the headiness of being wanted, the longing for the man she'd once loved slowly creeping out of its hiding place.

No.

That feeling had no place here. She and Antonio had made a pact as mature adults. Just a little over a week of pure pleasure and then they would part ways.

Although, she acknowledged as he reached down and tugged at the towel, a week didn't seem like nearly long enough.

The towel fell to the floor. Antonio stood there in all his naked glory. Her breath caught in her chest. She'd gotten glimpses of his arms, his chest, his abdomen over the past week. His legs were thick, similarly muscled and dusted with dark hair. Between his legs, his erection jutted out.

"There's a question on your face." He spoke the words softly, as if he was afraid he might spook her.

"You just…um…" She bit her lower lip. "You look really big."

His chuckle hummed through her. *"Gracías, mariposa."*

Something flickered across his face when he said her nickname. Before she could decipher it, he climbed on the bed, caging her between his arms, and leaned down to kiss her once more. She arched up, trying to press her nearly naked body against him, but only found cool air. Every time she lifted her hips, he stayed just out of reach, smiling against her lips.

"For a virgin, you're awfully eager," he said as he nipped her jaw.

"Have all your other virgins been terrified of *that*?" she asked, pointing to his hardness.

He went down on his elbows, his chest grazing hers, and cupped her face in his hands. The tender look in his eyes spoke to that current of longing, pulled it closer to the surface. He leaned over and pressed another kiss to her lips. "I want to take this slow. If you're going to give me the honor of being your first, I want to make it memorable."

She blinked rapidly to keep the tears at bay. She wouldn't be making a good case for her ability to stay emotionally detached if she cried before they'd even had sex.

"Well...thank you."

He chuckled then sank to press his body flush against hers. The sensuality of feeling his naked skin, of being able to run her hands over his arms, his back, up his neck and into his hair to bring his face back to hers for a more intense kiss, thrilled her.

Slowly, he kissed his way along her neck, back over her breasts. He cupped them in his hands, brought them to his mouth and nipped and licked all over with excruciating thoroughness, before continuing over her belly.

When his fingers settled on the edge of her thong, he paused. She looked at him and caught her breath. His eyes burned, dark mahogany in flames.

"I want to taste you."

Thank goodness she was lying down, because otherwise her knees would have collapsed at his words. She nodded once. His fingers skimmed beneath the material, slowly rolled it down her hips and over her thighs as he continued to press kisses to the sensitive skin of her legs.

And then she was just as naked as he was. Shy-

EMMY GRAYSON 171

ness crept in but didn't have time to linger and spread as Antonio moved back up her body. His hands settled on her thighs, gently parted them. Anticipation kept her body strung taut as a bowstring. When he kissed her *there*, her hips lifted off the bed as she cried out.

"*Antonio!*"

How was it possible to feel such pleasure? His tongue drove her mad, spiraling her higher and higher. She should be embarrassed to have her most intimate places bared to him, but it felt too good, felt too right, for her to dwell on that when the ecstasy was building with such intensity she could barely catch her breath.

The pleasure burst and she cried out his name again, her hands fisting in his hair as her hips pumped against his mouth. Then, slowly, her body dipped back to the bed as she went limp, cocooned by Antonio's warmth on top of her and the silk of his bed beneath her. Her eyes drifted shut as a smile curved her lips. She'd deal with the emotions later, because they were most certainly there, stronger than before, circling in the wake of the most intense passion she'd ever experienced.

Later. Because right now she was going to be glad she took the risk. For the rest of her life, she would never regret asking Antonio to take her to bed. Not when he'd given her such an incredible gift.

"That was…"

"Just the beginning."

Her eyes flew open to see him tearing open a condom packet. He sheathed his hard length, his gaze never leaving hers. She started to sit up. Curiosity and a hint of wickedness made her reach out and wrap her fingers around him. His breath hissed out. Before she could explore further, he tumbled her back onto the comforter.

"Later." Another searing kiss that rekindled the flames in her body. "Right now, I want to be inside you."

She swallowed hard, nodded. His hardness touched the delicate folds where his mouth had just been, her flesh even more sensitive. She arched up against him and he groaned, pushing slightly inside her.

Huh. She'd always heard the first time hurt, but this didn't, it felt naughty and sensual and so—

"Oh!"

As he slid further in, a pressure built, followed by a stinging sensation. This time her cry was sharp as her hands grabbed onto his arms and she winced.

"I'm sorry, Anna." He paused, kissing her forehead. "Do you want me to stop?"

"No, just…" She sucked in a shuddering breath. "Hurts."

"I've heard there can be pain sometimes, yes."

"Okay. Okay." Another breath. "Just…slow."

His head came down, his lips brushing her temple as he whispered something in Spanish. The deep timbre of his voice wound around her, the lilting phrases of his native tongue relaxing her taut muscles and distracting her from the pain. Each movement of his body was accompanied by a kiss. By the time he'd slid fully inside her, he'd kissed every inch of her face, from the tip of her nose to the shell of her ear.

"How does this feel?"

She wiggled around a little, adjusting to the sensation. He grimaced.

"Did I hurt you?" she asked, her hand coming up to rest on his jaw.

"Not in the way you're thinking. I'm trying to hold back so I don't hurt you."

She wiggled again, savoring the flare in his eyes. Plus, the ache had started to fade, the pleasure returning in a slow but steady current that spread throughout her body. She reached down and let her hands rest on his hips.

"I want to feel more."

His eyes darkened to almost black. One more kiss. One deep, soul-searing, mind-numbing kiss.

Then he began to move, sliding in and out of her with growing intensity. Each thrust went deeper. Their bodies moved into a natural rhythm, her hips arching up as he pulsed inside her. She savored his muscles flexing beneath her hands, the heat of his body, the feel of him inside her. The sensation collided with the carnal knowledge of what they were doing, the intimacy of their bodies being joined, that she was giving him as much pleasure as he was her.

The pressure began to build. She spread her legs wider to feel him even deeper inside her.

"Anna…"

Hearing her name whispered lit a fuse inside her core. Her arms flew around him, her fingers digging into his back.

"Antonio…please… I'm…"

His thrusts quickened, deepened. She was on the verge of something incredible, so close, almost…

"Antonio!"

His name burst from her lips as her body came apart in a blinding rush. He captured her breath with a kiss. She moaned against him, her body shuddering, quaking, the pleasure so intense, she almost couldn't take it.

He drove into her one last time. A groan escaped him as he found his release. Slowly, he lowered his body back onto hers, propping himself up on his elbows as he kissed her lightly, his lips tracing over hers in a soft, sweet kiss.

"That…that was…"

He lifted his head and smiled down at her. Another true smile, one that nearly broke her heart after the intimacy they had just shared. What would it be like to share this kind of affection with him day after day?

Stop.

She focused on the little tendrils of satisfaction still drifting through her body, the hazy warmth permeating her consciousness.

"That was amazing," she finally said.

"I'm glad I could impress."

"I'm also glad we agreed to a week of this." She couldn't imagine only sampling this once.

His smile flickered, disappearing for a split second before reappearing as he smoothed sweat-dampened wisps of hair off her face.

"Have I created a monster?"

No, he hadn't created a monster. But she might have unleashed one. She had severely underestimated her ability to stay detached, to enjoy sex without letting her emotions get in the way.

"No. I guess I just like sex."

With a laugh and another peck to her cheek, he got up and disappeared into the bathroom. She lay on the bed, the cool air swooping in to press down on her heated skin and whisk away the fantasy she'd briefly indulged in. How had she ever thought she was truly over him? If things had continued the way they had before their kiss yesterday, she could have convinced herself that he was too different from the boy she'd fallen for, that he had no interest in her and they were better off severing this briefly rekindled relationship after Alejandro and Calandra's wedding.

But knowing that he had wanted her, that he

had rejected her out of some misguided act of chivalry, sharing her body with him...

How was she supposed to just let that go?

Because he told you how things stand. This time around, at least, he'd been nothing but honest with her.

Mostly honest, she amended as she stood and grimaced at the ache between her legs. The scar... whatever had changed him from the boy he'd been at the beginning of summer to the man who'd broken her heart at the end was still a mystery.

The sound of water running drew her from the past. Antonio stepped out of the bathroom, still completely naked. With the sun shining in from the balcony, his skin looked like it was lit from within, a golden tan that, coupled with his black hair, made her think of a dark angel.

"Would you like to join me?"

He extended a hand, one eyebrow arched up at a rakish angle. Her body stirred.

She had a little over a week to enjoy what he was offering. A week, if she didn't muck it up with her naïve fantasies. Antonio had already shared so much with her that she hadn't known before. If he'd wanted to share what else had happened that summer, he would have already done so.

Time to be a big girl.

She raised her chin and smiled.

"I'd love to."

She accepted his hand, loved the way his fingers closed over hers possessively as he tugged her toward the shower.

Hot water cascaded from a waterfall shower that fogged the glass doors and created an intimate haven. He lathered her body with a woodsy-smelling soap, taking special care to wash the remnants of her first lovemaking off her thighs as he cradled her in his strong arms. This time, when he pulled on a condom and slid inside her, her body welcomed him as he lifted her up, wrapped her legs around his waist and pressed her against the wall.

Beneath the steaming water, he made love to her again, drawing out each thrust and teasing her until she dug her nails into his shoulders and begged for a release. He obliged by quickening his pace and reaching between their bodies, his fingers finding the sensitive bud above where their bodies were joined and stroking it until she came apart in his arms.

CHAPTER FIFTEEN

ANTONIO HIT END and cut off Alejandro's incessant questioning. His brother had called to confirm that Antonio and his "girlfriend" would be present at the rehearsal dinner the following day. A ruse, Antonio had discovered too late, for his brother to pester him with questions about Anna.

"So the tabloids were true," Alejandro had said with a laugh that had grated across Antonio's nerves.

"I don't kiss and tell. Unlike some people I know," he had shot back. His brothers didn't know about the ruse. God willing, they wouldn't find out. They had come through for him years ago with William's accident, making sure nothing had been leaked to the press and that their parents were kept in the dark. Adrian, already a moneymaking machine at that point, had covered all of William's care, from his time in the hospital to the lengthy physical therapy. When Antonio had made his own first six-figure deposit into his account, he had sent Adrian an amount he'd estimated would cover all of William's expenses. Adrian had tried to return it, but it was one of the few things Antonio had stood up to the eldest Cabrera sibling on.

Although, it wasn't like he and his brothers were close. Not only had their recent interest in matrimony and family driven them apart, but he'd always kept himself distant from them since the accident. He'd been sick with guilt and, eventually, ashamed that he'd fallen into the traditional baby brother role of needing his older siblings to bail him out. That he'd also put their hard-earned reputations at risk, as well having to rely on Adrian's money initially to do the right thing by William, had killed him.

Too bad, he reflected as he walked back into the restaurant. Because he could sure as hell use someone to talk to right about now. He stalked up the stairs, his heartbeat kicking into overdrive as he neared the top.

She was waiting for him up there. Their last night in Positano. Tomorrow was the rehearsal dinner. Saturday, the wedding. Sunday, the post-wedding breakfast.

And then it would be over. Anna would depart for Paris and begin to sew as if her life depended on it. Five more requests had come in over the last week, along with offers from several major brands and influencers. The more their photos appeared in magazines, Instagram feeds and enter-

tainment talk shows, the more her inbox piled up.
Her friend Kess had hopped on several conference
calls, providing guidance on which designers and
shows Anna should focus on.

Their charade had continued to prove successful for him, too. The more they'd wandered Positano, the more *Le Porto* had cropped up. His head
of marketing had yakked on and on about their social media metrics, excitement vibrating through
the phone on their last call.

Still, in the last couple of days, he'd noticed
fewer photographers and mentions of their romance and more of Alejandro's upcoming wedding. If he and Anna staged it right, they could
continue the pretense of their relationship continuing past the wedding. Flowers delivered to
her apartment in Paris, an occasional "mention"
to the press by a discreet friend who gushed about
how much fun they were having.

It had all fallen into place despite his lack of
planning.

He reached the top of the stairs and walked
onto the rooftop terrace of the restaurant perched
on the mountaintops overlooking Positano, Capri
and the Galli Isles. He'd reserved the entire terrace for privacy. At least, that's what he'd told
Anna when he'd surprised her with the limo ride
up the mountainside.

But in reality, he wanted her all to himself. A
notion he was glad he'd paid attention to because

when she'd walked out into the living area of the penthouse earlier this evening, possession had sunk its talons into his skin.

Mine.

The dress hung from her shoulders by silver-braided threads, the straps holding up a gossamer fabric the color of lilacs. The plunging neckline and thin strip of sheer material wrapped around her waist had given him a glimpse of bare skin before falling into a wide, fluffy skirt that stopped just below her knees. Flowers and ivy vines crawled over the bodice. A nod to her love of the outdoors, she'd shared with him.

Now she sat by the terrace railing, the evening light creating an enchanting glow that catapulted the entire scene from beautiful to stunning. The private table, set with a deep blue tablecloth, boasted plates of rice balls stuffed with tomato sauce, mozzarella and peas, and wineglasses filled with Barbaresco. A candle flickered romantically in the center next to a small vase of orange-colored blossoms. The view of the mountain, craggy outcroppings and cascading slopes tumbling into the ocean seemed almost too perfect to be real. The Italian cities he wished they had more time to explore twinkled below.

Yet the one thing that stood out to him in the midst of all that splendor was Anna. The sparkle in her eyes. The smile lingering on her lips. How she still looked so sweet despite the many lessons in debauchery he'd given her the past week.

Guilt crept up on him, fast and venomous. The magic dimmed a little. All week, he'd been ignoring his conscience. Mornings had still been reserved for work, but as noon had drawn near, he'd found himself walking quicker and quicker to the penthouse to collect Anna.

Before he'd made love to her, they'd made their way down to the lobby in an efficient manner. Now he hurried to be by her side, linger on the balcony as she showed him the sketches and samples she'd put together that day. He loved watching her eyes light up, looking at the pictures of what had inspired her that morning, and offering suggestions here and there when she asked. Or sharing his own ideas for where he wanted his business to go and she'd asked questions, showed enthusiasm for his aspirations. That was one thing that hadn't changed about her. She'd always been interested in him just for him, not for his name or wealth. He'd loved how she'd cared more for flowers picked on a mountainside than all the exotic blooms his money could buy.

Love.

His step faltered. That word had cropped up more and more throughout the past week. He couldn't pinpoint the moment he'd gone from living in the moment to thinking of the future. A future he had never before contemplated; at least, not one with a woman in it. But now when he thought of the future, he couldn't see one without Anna in it.

What would she say if he told her all? Over the past few days, she'd slowly drawn out details he hadn't shared with anyone. How he felt even more estranged from his brothers in recent months. Anna, bless her, hadn't coddled him or backed down. No, that newfound fire had surged forth once more and she'd challenged him to talk to them after Alejandro's honeymoon.

"You've put up the walls," she'd said. "So why not tear them down if it's making you unhappy?"

She'd accepted everything so far. If he told her about the accident, about the guilt he'd been carrying around for so long, would she stay? Could confession be the first step toward a life that meant something more? Toward healing not only himself but his relationships with his brothers? With Anna? Maybe even William?

Anna looked up, her smile falling when she saw his face.

"Is everything okay?"

"Everything's fine," he said, leaning down to kiss her. Another selfish indulgence, but one he'd embraced gladly. The first day they'd gone out after spending the previous afternoon and evening in bed together, Anna had curled into his side and wrapped an arm around his waist with an intimate ease that had both terrified and thrilled him. Aware that photographers could be hiding anywhere, he'd allowed it. As the day had progressed, he'd found himself responding in kind, kissing her cheek, reaching out for her hand.

It wasn't just sex with Anna. No, it was the intimacy, the familiarity, that made his time with her so enjoyable. He hadn't felt like himself in a long while, but she dragged it out of him, made him relax.

He sat across from her and picked up his wineglass, watching the candlelight play over the ruby-red liquid.

"Alejandro called to confirm tomorrow."

She grimaced. "I'm not looking forward to that."

"Why not? You'll get to see your aunt and uncle. My family's looking forward to seeing you, too."

"And that'll be nice. It's just…" She bit down on her lower lip. A habit, he'd noticed, when she was worried about something.

"Just what?" he asked, reaching across the table and capturing her hand in his. She slowly breathed out.

"I don't like lying to our families."

"I don't, either. But it won't hurt them in the long run."

One bare shoulder rose and fell in a shrug. "True. It's not like we're pretending to be engaged or something."

His eyes dropped to the diamond bracelet on

her wrist. What would it be like to put another type of diamond on her hand?

"I'm also surprised at how easily my family accepted the story of us dating," Anna continued, oblivious to his inner turmoil. "They were intrusive, almost obsessive, about who I dated in college. But they've barely talked to me the past two weeks."

He kept his expression neutral. The couple of times he'd been in touch with Diego, the butler had been surprisingly overjoyed at the thought of Anna and Antonio dating. Antonio hadn't been able to bring himself to tell Diego that it was all a lie.

"They knew you and I were close as children. I wouldn't read too much into it."

She squeezed his hand and gave him another heart-stopping smile. "You're probably right. No sense worrying about it right now when we have this view." A dimple flashed in her cheek.

He tried to refocus, to enjoy the rest of their evening. But their brief conversation about the wedding, the impending deadline on their fake relationship, clouded his earlier happiness. Even seeing Anna's eyes widen in delight at the dessert, lemon sorbet drizzled with red raspberry sauce and topped with fresh mint leaves, did little to assuage his bad mood. He was at a crossroads. He could tell Anna and risk her rejection.

Or she could accept him, ugly past and all. He didn't know which of the two frightened him more.

The ride down the mountain increased his impending sense of doom. His driver took a curve a touch too fast, the move making Anna fall against him as his heart thundered in his chest. He'd slept next to Anna every night the last six nights. Each morning, he'd awoken nightmare-free. Another sign, he thought, that perhaps his time with Anna was healing the past.

But now, as the car moved back into its lane and continued on, adrenaline pumped through his veins as tires screeched in his mind and William cried out.

Anna, bless her, looked out the window, soaking in the sights and thankfully missing the past burrowing its way back under his skin.

He helped her out of the car back at the hotel. She smiled at the freshly painted flowers and now working fountain, the water splashing down in a tinkling melody. She'd mentioned it to him the other day, about how she looked forward to seeing the final results. He'd paid triple for a local gardener to come in and plant an array of lush blooms, as well as a bonus to the construction workers to get the fountain working before Thursday evening.

Before they left. Because he'd wanted Anna to see it. Not because it was a practical business decision or because it was a necessity. No, he'd done something spur-of-the-moment just because he'd wanted to make her happy.

The elevator ground to a halt. Antonio swore and punched a button.

Paul's voice filled the small space, smooth and refined. "Yes, sir?"

"Paul, the elevator's stuck."

"One moment, sir." A crackle of static, followed by, "Sir, one of the construction crews stayed late. They shut down the elevator to work on something. It'll be just a minute."

He ground his teeth. He wasn't paying one of the top construction firms in Italy as much as he was to have them—

Anna's hands moved up over his chest, grabbed onto the lapels of his suit jacket and pulled him down for a kiss. His arms wrapped around her, a habit now when she kissed him. She tasted sweet, like lemons and raspberries.

She nibbled on his lower lip, eliciting a groan. The first two days, he'd been adamant that she allow him to teach her, to go slow and savor each moment. But once he'd allowed her to sink to her knees in the shower and take his length in her mouth, he'd been lost. Anna approached lovemaking with the same carefree joy and curious adventurousness she approached life with. It was intoxicating.

"Might as well make the most of our time," she whispered against his mouth with a smile.

She had no idea the battle raging inside him. But her words hit hard. They had one night left before they joined the rest of the family in Marseilles. One more night to enjoy her body before he had to make the most critical decision of his life. He might have a lifetime of this kind of pleasure with her...or this might be the last time.

The thought of another man touching her, kissing her, made his hands tighten on her waist and pull her body against his. She gasped, arched against him. His fingers tangled in her hair and, with a gentle tug, he tilted her head back, baring her neck to his lips. He trailed kisses along her throat to the beautifully tanned skin of her breasts swelling past that seductively plunging neckline.

One hand drifted up, the diamond bracelet winking under the lights of the elevator. With a tug, the bodice sagged, the straps sliding down her arms to reveal her bare breasts. His lust became a living thing, pulsing in his veins as he dipped his head and sucked a pebbled peak into his mouth. He kept one hand on her waist, the other drifting up to cup her other breast and tease the nipple with his thumb. Her fingers delved into his hair, frantic, as her breathing quickened, the sound urging him on. He glanced up to see her eyes closed, lashes dark against her skin, rosy lips parted as she panted. His gaze drifted to the mirrored walls behind her, the reflection of his seductive foreplay and her passionate response reflected a hundred times all around them.

"Open your eyes, Anna. Watch."

Her lashes swept up. Pink tinged her cheekbones as she smiled shyly at the mirrors. God, he loved that about her. How, even after everything he'd introduced her to, she could still be so innocent.

As he continued to lavish attention on her breasts, he caught her gaze in the mirror, held it. Her smile turned daring as her touch drifted away from his hair, down his back and then around front. He felt her fingers on his trousers, heard the hiss of his zipper and then groaned as she reached in and wrapped her fingers around him.

He calculated the likelihood of how long it would take Paul to reach the construction workers and get the elevator moving. Probably too soon for him to make love to her the way he wanted to, but not too soon for him to still make her come apart in his arms.

He reached down, fisted her skirts and lifted the frothy material. Her eyes glazed over as his fingers slipped inside the silk thong she'd donned for the evening.

So wet, so hot.

He rubbed her silken flesh, watched her face as he slipped a finger inside her molten heat. She writhed against him, moaning his name. Her hand tightened on his hardness, but before she could start the rhythm that had undone him two nights ago, he pulled her hand away, grabbed her arm and lifted it above her head. He paused in his sensual ministrations to her core and captured her other arm, pinning both above her head in his grasp.

He would remember her like this forever. Hair tumbling down over her shoulders, her naked breasts barely visible through the dark curtain, lips swollen and eyes alight with desire for him.

He leaned in, kissed her as he reached back under her skirts, slipped a finger inside and savored the clench of her muscles around him. He slid in and out, brushing his thumb over her most sensitive place, savoring the hitch in her breath, the scent of her passion curling around him and making him feel like a god for bringing her such pleasure.

"Antonio, please."

He wanted to drag out the moment, tease her, savor the feel of her as he gazed in the mirrors and saw every single angle of their bodies pressed together.

But he had no desire for Paul or any of the construction workers to see Anna like this. Because then he'd have to kill them.

He quickened his pace, stroking his finger in and out as he lovingly massaged her. When she came, his name escaped her lips on a cry as she shuddered against him, her head dropping to his shoulder. He turned his head, pressed a quick kiss to her temple, then slid the straps of her dress up to cover her once more.

Not a moment too soon. With a grinding of gears, the elevator jerked back into motion. Paul's voice came back on.

"Is it working, sir?"

"Yes. Good night, Paul."

A breathy laugh sounded against his throat. "Are there cameras in here?"

"Not yet. Next week."

Dios mío. He hadn't even considered that they might be recorded.

Because you weren't thinking with your brain.

He glanced down at Anna as she straightened the straps of her dress, smoothed her hair and shot him a thousand-watt smile that rivaled the brightness of the mini chandelier overhead. Being with her, thinking about everything but what was safe, made him reckless.

His feelings for her had made him reckless once before. He felt differently now, more in control… but what if he hadn't really changed?

Enough. Time for self-contemplation later.

When the elevator doors opened, he scooped her up in his arms and carried her down the hall and across the threshold. She threw back her head and laughed. He laid her on the bed, climbed up next to her and covered her body with his, his fingers cupping the back of her head as he kissed her deeply. He started to pull the straps down once more. But before he could bare her breasts to his gaze, she shimmied out from under him and darted over to the doors leading out to the balcony.

"May I share a secret with you?"

That shyness killed him every time. With other women, he might have assumed it was an act, an attempt to be coy. But not his Anna.

"Given how much you've shared with me this week, I think I can handle one secret."

"The first time you kissed me…" Her hand fluttered toward the far end of the balcony. "When you put me up on the table…"

He rolled off the bed and stalked toward her, enjoying the quickening rise and fall of her chest.

"Vividly."

He reached her side but didn't touch her, heightening the anticipation.

"I imagined you laying me down on the table and making love to me."

It was the first time either of them had said the words "make love" out loud. He noted her blink, the quick disconnect as her mind scrambled to come up with an alternative term.

"I mean, have se—"

He cut her off, wrapping his arms around her, lifting her up and tossing her over his shoulder. Her laugh filled the night air, melodic and sweet.

"Antonio! What are you doing?"

"Fulfilling your wish, *mariposa*."

He flipped a switch on the wall. Lights Paul had insisted on being installed among the ivy lit up, creating an intimate glow. He made a mental note to give Paul a raise as he set Anna down and watched her look around the balcony with awe.

"This is beautiful." Her smile landed on him. "I'm really happy for you, Antonio. This place is going to be so successful."

Pride swelled in his chest. No one outside his family had shown any interest in his hotels, other than to inquire about free rooms or how much money his properties raked in.

"Thank you, Anna."

Before she could reply, he slid his fingers under the straps of her dress, tugging the material down over her body. As the fabric peeled away, he pressed kisses to her heated skin, delighting in the sounds she made for him. By the time he'd finished, she was panting, her skin flushed with desire. He scooped up her naked body, laid her out on the table. She watched as he undressed, slowly, teasing her as he took his time unbuttoning his shirt, sliding off his slacks and rolling a condom onto his hard length.

He started to join her on the table, but she sat up and shook her head.

"Lay down."

He nearly came right then and there. He laid back on the table, watched with bated breath as she straddled his hips. She braced her hands against his shoulders. Then, with aching slowness, she lowered herself onto him, eyes closing as she moaned. As she found her tempo, he met her body with his own thrusts. When she found her release and cried out, he reached up, his hand tangling in her hair and bringing her head down for a kiss. He followed a moment later, his body shaking as his climax shuddered through him.

Anna collapsed on top of him. He stroked his hand up and down her back, savoring the feel of her body against his. He took mental note of everything: the silken caress of her hair against his face, the heated dampness of her skin, the freckles dotting her nose.

No matter how the weekend ended, he would remember this for the rest of his life.

CHAPTER SIXTEEN

THE SOFT STRAINS of a romantic song drifted across the deck of the ship. A dance floor had been cordoned off by lights strung up above the wood decking. Couples swayed together, dressed in a sea of vividly colored gowns and ebony suits. In the midst of the crowd, Alejandro and his bride, Calandra, had eyes only for each other.

Anna smiled down into her champagne glass. Who would have thought the boy she'd once spied filling the sleeves of the British ambassador's coat with shaving cream would end up married to someone as straitlaced and put together as Calandra?

Her gaze lifted, drifted over the crowd. Antonio had disappeared after the dinner. The few times she'd spied him, he'd been talking with men who looked very important, the kind who were still answering emails during the ceremony held in the grand ballroom below.

Apprehension pricked her skin. Ever since she'd woken up yesterday morning to an empty bed and a brief note saying Antonio would meet her in Marseille, she'd known. The fairy tale they'd created the last week had been over. Paul had conveyed that Antonio had had to take the helicopter and help his brother.

"Last-minute wedding details," he'd told her.

The twist of his lips beneath his magnificent moustache had told her he hadn't believed Antonio's excuse, either.

When she'd arrived at Alejandro's villa, it had been to find her aunt and uncle eagerly waiting for her. Instead of the worried frowns that normally carved wrinkles into their expressions, they'd been glowing with happiness. They'd gushed over her, the requests that had been pouring in for her design portfolio and, of course, her relationship. Aunt Lonita, especially, had peppered her with questions. She'd nearly swooned when Antonio had shown up to escort them all to dinner on the lawn where a long banquet table had been set for the Cabrera family and rehearsal guests.

He'd played the part well. Whenever people asked if Anna had been his secret girlfriend all along, he'd smiled coyly, saying what mattered was that she was with him now, as he pressed a kiss to her fingers.

Hollow. She'd sensed the distance behind the gestures, observed the tightness around his eyes. It hadn't surprised her that he hadn't visited her room last night, or that he'd kept his distance until the reception when he'd escorted her into dinner.

She took a long drink of champagne. It was what they'd agreed to. She'd been mentally preparing herself for it the closer and closer they'd gotten. But she would have rather he just disappear after their last night of lovemaking than continue with the pretense in front of their family and friends.

She looked up from her glass and stretched her lips into a smile as her uncle approached.

"Enjoying the reception?" he asked, his eyes twinkling beneath his bushy brows.

"I am."

Another lie. She'd always heard once one lie was uttered the others stacked up faster than they could be tracked.

Diego glanced around. "Where's your beau?"

"Antonio? Um…talking with someone about business, I think."

His eyes settled back on her. An ache formed in her chest. Over the years, she'd gotten used to seeing his blue eyes, so like her mother's. But right now, when she desperately missed and wanted her mom to hug her, to tell her everything was going to be okay as she cried on her shoulder, it hurt to see the reminder of what she'd lost.

"Why do I think there's something you're not telling me?"

Her pulse skipped a beat. "What?"

"You were never good at lying, Anna."

"I…that is, we…"

Where was Antonio when she needed him? Much as she detested the suave, professional side of him, he would be able to talk their way out of this.

"You looked very happy in the photos your aunt and I saw." His head tilted to one side. "You don't look so happy now."

"I'm sorry about the photos, Tío." The one detail she could latch onto and discuss without spinning more falsehoods. "I should have given you and Aunt Lonita more of a heads-up. Everything just happened so fast."

Her uncle chuckled. "We were surprised, but not shocked. I'm more surprised it took the two of you so long to figure things out."

Panic started to claw at her throat. She knew she'd only be able to keep up the pretense so long.

"What do you mean?"

"You were so close when you were younger. He was the only one I trusted with you. I can't believe he didn't snatch you up sooner." Concern deepened the wrinkles in his face. "But something doesn't seem right. You disappear to Paris to focus on your design career. You run off to Rome with a friend from college. Then you appear in the tabloids with the youngest son of my employer."

She winced. "I'm sorry. I didn't mean to make you worry."

Diego's thick brows drew together. "I know."

"It's just… I know you and Tía Lonita worry about me."

He leaned against the railing of the ship. "We do." He sighed. "Too much, I'm afraid."

Her mouth dropped open. "What?"

Diego looked out over the black waters of the Gulf of Lion, his expression darkening. "When you came to Spain, you were so afraid. Every time Lonita and I went out, I remember coming home and seeing you at the top of the stairs, waiting for us."

Her hands tightened around her champagne glass. She hadn't realized her aunt and uncle had observed her.

"I was afraid, too." His words were spoken so softly, she almost didn't hear them. "But I think I used your fear as an excuse to act more like a dictator than your uncle. We put guidelines and boundaries into place. To make you feel safer." Diego's blue gaze landed on her. "But we made it worse." He reached out, his bearlike hand resting on her shoulder. "I never wanted you to fear another day in your life. But when I saw the photos of you in Rome, then with Antonio, the joy on your face compared to how you grew up around us…" He swallowed hard, his eyes glistening. "I realized how much I'd hurt you."

Tears stung her eyes, hot and fierce.

"I thought you didn't trust me," she finally whispered.

"As much as it pains me to say this, it had little to do with you and everything to do with how I reacted to losing my little sister. The more I took charge, the more in control I felt."

Her free hand gripped the railing of the ship and she stared out over the darkness of a night-shrouded Mediterranean Sea.

"I felt so lost after Mom and Dad died," she finally whispered. "Lost, and like I was drowning in fear." Tears spilled over. "I said goodbye that night, but I didn't kiss Mom. I was too busy watching a show." Her hand drifted up, touched her forehead. "But she kissed me. Right here. And then, twenty minutes later, she was just...gone."

Diego's hand settled over hers on the railing. "I was happy you and Antonio became friends. He was always a good boy, responsible. And he seemed to do the one thing I couldn't." When she glanced up at him, he smiled. "He made you happy."

Her lips quirked. "Everyone else treated me like glass. Antonio was the only one who didn't. When we walked out onto the mountain that first time..." Her voice trailed off as memory assailed her. The velvety softness of the lush green grass cradling her bare feet. The breeze carrying the faint scent of earth. A boy holding her hand and tugging her forward, pulling her out of the dark hole she'd tumbled into. "It was like I'd been holding my breath ever since I'd been told about their deaths and I could suddenly breathe again."

"We were very grateful for him." She glanced up to see Diego's eyes glinting in the moonlight, as if he, too, were fighting back tears. "He did what Lonita and I couldn't."

"So you…you didn't think I was too immature? Incapable?"

"No. Just the opposite, Anna. To lose your parents and travel across the world to live with relatives you'd only met a handful of times? I thought you were one of the most resilient and strong, young women I'd ever met. We just didn't want you to hurt anymore, and horribly enough, we did just that by trying to protect you."

She nearly dropped her champagne glass as she sagged against the railing. How had they not had this conversation in all these years?

"I'm sorry, Anna." Her uncle brushed a fatherly kiss against her cheek. "But look at how far you've come, despite everything Lonita and I did."

"With good intention—" she started to say, but Diego cut her off.

"Intentions, at least in this case, don't absolve us of the sins we committed."

"Perhaps. But after…" She'd started to say *after Antonio's rejection*, but she wasn't quite ready to share that humiliation just yet. "After graduation, those restrictions were safe, a cocoon from the real world. Even my job in Granada had been safe, a way to indulge in my love of fashion without risking rejection."

He chuckled. "We all do things like that, find ways to not confront the more challenging parts of ourselves. But you broke free, Anna. When you lost your job, I was ready to step in, take care of everything."

"I know," she said with a smile. Amazing how just a few minutes of conversation transformed her emotions about the moment she'd told her aunt and uncle "thank you but no," she was moving to Paris, and seen the twin looks of horror and listened with quiet anger to their warnings of all the bad things that could happen.

"I was scared. But despite my fear, I was proud, too." His eyes crinkled at the corners as he smiled. "Your mother would be, too."

Warmth bloomed in her chest She'd taken more risks in the past six months than she had in thirteen years. Never in her wildest dreams would she have imagined moving to Paris or walking in a professional fashion show in Rome, much less inviting her childhood love to be her first lover.

But she had. And each risk had resulted in something incredible. Her own apartment covered from floor to ceiling in *her* designs. Walking the runway and having her work seen by the public for the first time. A week of the most incredible physical pleasure she'd ever experienced, of loving and being loved by Antonio.

Because she did love him. She probably hadn't ever stopped loving him, not fully. But the last week had pulled those suppressed emotions back to the surface. Not just the sex, although, she acknowledged with a rueful smile, that had certainly helped.

No, it had been seeing the man Antonio had grown into emerge from beneath the façade he presented to the rest of the world. The pride he took in his work. The way he remembered the names of the construction workers and interior designers scuttling around the hotel, holding them to his standard yet still complimenting their work and remembering that the foreman's daughter had just started college. How he'd asked questions about her work, shown interest, encouraged her to fully embrace what she loved to design. How he'd finally started to share the ghosts of his past, to trust her once more with his secrets. He still held something back, but she could be patient, wait and support him while he came to terms with whatever had altered his life so drastically. He was worth it.

The boy she'd fallen for had turned into a man she loved very deeply.

Resolve took hold of her. Perhaps it was time to take one more risk. If he rejected her again, the result would be the same as if she kept quiet; Antonio would be out of her life after tomorrow.

She set her glass down on a passing tray and wrapped her arms around Diego's tall frame.

"I love you, Tío."

Diego hugged her back.

Her eyes grew heavy with the weight of more tears that she thankfully blinked away. "Thank you." She stepped back. "If you'll excuse me, I need to go find Antonio."

Questions appeared in Diego's eyes, but he only nodded. She turned and almost ran into a woman standing right behind her.

"Oh, I'm sorry…" Her voice trailed off as her eyes widened. "You…you're…"

The woman smiled, red-painted lips curving up. A pixie haircut kept her silver hair short and slicked back from her face, except for a dusting of fringe that lay on her smooth forehead. Her expression was friendly, but the green eyes that assessed her from behind black circular frames were shrewd and alert. "Sylvie Smythe."

Legendary designer. Queen of fashion.

"It's an honor, Ms. Smythe," she managed to choke out.

Sylvie nodded her head with the regal aplomb of a queen. Her eyes darted to Diego, who still stood by the railing.

"May I have a moment of your time, Miss Vega?"

Anna nodded to Diego to let him know she was

okay. Then Sylvie's words registered and her head snapped back around as Diego walked off.

"You know my name?"

"The Virgin Designer."

Her stomach dropped. Would she ever escape that horrid article?

Sylvie leaned in. "Leo White doesn't know anything about fashion, and even less about women."

"Oh. Well, he was—"

"Rude. And a bastard."

Anna choked on a laugh. "Yes."

"But he did do one thing right. He brought you to my attention."

Don't panic, don't panic. "You looked at my portfolio?"

"Yes. I'd like to think I would have looked at your portfolio regardless, but…" She shrugged. "The important thing is I did." Sylvie glanced down at Anna's dress. "One of yours?"

"Yes."

Sylvie walked around her in a circle, assessing the violet-hued, strapless gown. Anna stood frozen to the spot, afraid to even take a breath.

Sylvie stopped in front of her. Her eyes traveled over every inch of the garment. At one point, she reached out, captured a piece of skirt between her fingers and rubbed the fabric.

"Exceptional. The one you wore in the article—" She made a face. "But this, the gold one in Rome, everything I've seen since…exceptional."

Dizzying elation spiraled through Anna as she fought to maintain a neutral expression.

"Thank you, ma'am."

"Sylvie, please. I didn't spend the last twenty years getting Botox to be called 'ma'am.'"

"Sylvie, then, I—"

"Have you entered into any agreements since you became famous?"

"Agreements?"

"Brands, department stores, boutiques."

"Oh. Um, no, I was going to make a decision next week."

Sylvie regarded her for another long moment.

Anna resisted squirming, meeting the older woman's gaze.

"What would you say if I asked you to reject all those other requests and start your own line with me?"

The world rocked under her feet.

"What?"

Sylvie took a phone out of the folds of her gown and pulled up a picture. She held it out to Anna, who accepted it with trembling hands. It was a picture of her on her first day in Positano outside the silk merchant stall wearing her cream sundress as she gazed at the red fabric with loving eyes.

"This is beautiful." Sylvie's gravelly voice softened. "This is the kind of dress that could make any woman feel beautiful, as she should." She took the phone from Anna's trembling fingers and hit another button. A collage of photos sprung up, each one from a tabloid showing Anna in the clothing she'd worn in Positano. "I want you to make these dresses for Sylvie Smythe."

Any moment now she was going to wake up and pinch herself because she had to be dreaming.

"I would love to. It's just…"

Sylvie's eyes narrowed. "What?"

"I want to make them the right way. I know making ethical clothing affordable can be challenging but it's important to me to be involved in the whole process, including sourcing the fabric and labor."

Sylvie's face smoothed into an unreadable expression. *The Botox probably helps with that*, Anna thought frantically. How unorthodox for a woman to be told by one of the most famous designers in the world that she was going to give her a chance, only to have that little nobody set terms and conditions of her own?

And then Sylvie smiled, an even bigger smile that made her radiant in all her silver splendor.

"I think you and I are going to get along very well, Miss Vega."

CHAPTER SEVENTEEN

THE INANE BLABBER coming from David Hill, the slightly inebriated hotel mogul next to Antonio, rolled off him as he kept an eye on Anna, who was now conversing with a silver-haired woman. A smile tugged at his lips, despite his best efforts, as pride rushed through him. He didn't recognize the woman on sight, but he'd asked David who she was, and he knew the name. If Sylvie Smythe had taken notice of Anna's work, it was only a matter of time before she became a household name.

David resumed his diatribe. His hands flew out as he described the site of his next hotel and nearly smacked Isabella Cabrera in the chest.

"David!" Antonio said sharply.

"It was an accident, Tony," Isabella said with a gracious smile for David, who had the good sense to look abashed.

"Still, my apologies, Isabella." He rubbed his palms against his suit jacket. "I think I'll go find some coffee."

He scuttled off before Antonio could chastise him further for nearly hitting the mother of the groom.

"I've never seen David so animated," Isabella remarked as she glided forward and hugged Antonio. Amazing how, even at twenty-nine years old, seeing his mother calmed him.

"Three glasses of champagne on an empty stomach probably had something to do with it."

Isabella laughed. "I'm surprised you're talking to him and not spending time with your lovely new girlfriend."

He tensed. Reintroducing Anna to his family yesterday had gone well. But he'd sensed Isabella's curious gaze scrutinizing them during dinner. The relentless slew of events had kept him busy all day. The post-rehearsal dinner drinks with the groom's party had lasted far longer than he'd anticipated, and he'd opted to sleep in a guest room in case he woke Anna up. He'd entertained the idea of sliding into bed with her, waking her up with long, languid kisses…

Much as he loathed the idea, they needed to talk first.

"She's talking with Sylvie Smythe."

"Oh! Is Sylvie interested in her work?" At his nod, she clapped her hands together. "How wonderful! You must be so excited for her."

"I am."

He felt more than saw his mother's eyes move over his face, searching for answers.

"Something's wrong."

A statement, not a question. Of course, Isabella would pick up on whatever was bothering him. She'd always been tuned in to whatever he and Alejandro had been thinking.

Before he could answer, Javier Cabrera walked up. Antonio had never been so grateful to see his father in all his life.

"Father."

Javier reached out and clasped his son's shoulder.

Antonio blinked in surprise. It was the closest Javier had come to hugging him. Ever.

"Son. Congratulations on your upcoming hotel."

Had he landed in an alternate reality? One where his father paid attention to his life?

"Thank you, sir."

Javier glanced at his wife. Antonio noted the beads of sweat on his brow, the shifting of his weight from one foot to another. It took a moment to dissect the motions as signs of nervousness. He'd never seen Javier as anything but unflappable, save for the one argument he'd overheard between Alejandro and Javier when Javier had allowed his anger to rule and raised his voice.

"Hello, dear."

He kissed his wife on the cheek. Isabella flashed him a strained smile. "Darling."

They stood there, the three of them, in a long

moment of awkward silence. Then Javier mumbled—*mumbled*—something about checking on the wedding cake, pressed another kiss to her cheek and disappeared into the crowd.

Antonio watched his father walk away then turned to his mother, one brow raised.

"What was that about?"

Isabella's smile was brittle. "Just some things your father and I are dealing with."

His mother had always had her head in the clouds every time she'd talked about her husband. Adrian and Alejandro had hinted at trouble the last time he'd seen them, but given Adrian's contentious history with their mother and Alejandro's ability to annoy their father just by walking into a room, he'd brushed it aside.

"Things?"

Isabella gazed at Alejandro and Calandra as Alejandro dipped her on the dance floor before bringing her back up to kiss her.

"I'm glad you and Anna have known each other so long." Her fingers curled so tightly around her wineglass, he was surprised it didn't shatter. "When you fall in love with a fairy tale and rush in without thinking, it's easier to get hurt."

Her words knifed through him, added a new worry. Had his last two weeks with Anna been real? Was what he felt for her real? If he asked her to actually be in a relationship, would they discover that, away from the glitz and glamor of Positano, he had created a fantasy built on the flimsy foundation of lust and old memories?

Or was he being a coward and throwing up roadblocks?

"Darling, I didn't mean to upset you." Isabella laid a hand on his cheek. "Your father and I will get through this. I'm so happy you and your brothers have found women who love you as much as they do."

His heart kicked into overdrive. "Love?"

Isabella smiled. "If she hasn't told you yet, she will soon. I saw the way she looked at you."

Words meant to assure, to bolster. But instead they dropped with lethal intensity, grabbing hold of his doubts and insecurities and inflating them until they were pressing in on him from all sides. Anna had kept her emotions in check, giving no hint that she'd cared for him other than as a friend or casual lover. Another reason the thought of talking with her scared the hell out of him. She'd survived, even thrived, despite the heartbreak he'd put her through. How would he handle such a rejection?

The selfishness of that thought hit him hard, swamped him in a tangled mire of guilt, fear and self-anger. He hadn't changed. Not really, not the way Anna had as she'd grown and blossomed. He'd taken her under his wing to fill the void left by Alejandro. He'd pressured his friend into joining him for a joy ride he hadn't wanted to go on so he could escape his own illicit desires. And he'd suggested this whole fake relationship to get the media off his back and make *him* feel better that he'd done something to help Anna.

Knowing he'd been right all along, that he didn't deserve the happiness Anna brought him, nearly knocked him off his feet.

Resolve straightened his spine. There would be no conversation with Anna, except to wish her well and thank her for helping him. And then he would set her free to find a man who deserved her. Even if it killed him.

He was about to excuse himself when a man walking along the deck caught his eye, cane in hand. His head was down, but Antonio knew him in an instant.

William.

William lifted his head. A jagged scar cut down his old friend's face. In one hand, he clutched a cane. Somehow, over the music, the conversation, the clink of glasses, Antonio could hear every fall of the cane on the deck, offset by the scraping of William's right foot that dragged slightly on the ground.

"Is that William?" Isabella asked, her voice excited. "Goodness, I wonder what happened. I haven't seen him in years. Do you two keep in… Antonio?"

He walked away, his mother's voice fading as he stalked toward the stern of the boat. He knew

Adrian and Alejandro had both kept in touch with William over the years. It shouldn't be a surprise that he would be there. If William still felt the same way he had when he'd written that letter, he would probably be at least cordial, if not friendly, if they ran into each other.

But Antonio was feeling too raw to deal with another piece of his past right now.

He reached the stern. Thankfully, the deck chairs and recently added pool were empty. Lights brought the water to life, ripples spreading over the surface from the barely perceptible rocking of the great ship.

Alone, he sucked in a deep breath, his lungs filling with salty sea air. It was no wonder William walked with a cane. His right leg had been pinned, blood darkening his jeans to almost black as Antonio had pried him from the wreckage, the overwhelming scent of leaking oil spurring him on to free his friend. He'd managed to drag William, half conscious and moaning in pain, back up to the road.

He'd already made his decision. Seeing William like this was just confirmation he was doing the right thing.

"Antonio?"

He closed his eyes, savored the sweet melody of her voice, before turning around.

She stood at the far end of the pool. Dear God, she looked just like a princess, a gown of deep purple clinging to her body before flaring out at her knees. The hemline kissed the deck and gave the impression that she was gliding rather than walking as she drew near.

"Are you okay?"

"Fine," he bit out. "I'd like to be alone."

She froze, uncertainty crossing her face. "Okay. I just—"

"You don't need to be here, Anna." He inhaled, mentally steeling himself for the task at hand. "After the wedding breakfast tomorrow, I'll arrange for your flight back to Paris on our jet."

She stared at him. "I saw William."

His throat tightened. Not what he'd expected her to say. But perhaps it was better this way.

"And?"

She tilted her head, her gaze piercing through his armor.

"That's it, isn't it?"

"What?" The harsh laugh that grated past his lips sounded cruel, as it was meant to. She had no way of knowing the source; the pain of his past combining with the anguish of losing sight of a future he'd never thought possible. "Find another reason if you want to, Anna, but our arrangement was through this weekend."

"Your mom mentioned William was in a car accident." He despised the pity he saw on her face. "Were you driving, Antonio? Is that what this is all about? You punishing yourself years later?"

"I'm not talking about this," he snapped. "We had our fun. Judging by your chat with Sylvie Smythe, the plan worked for you. It worked for me. End of story. Contract terminated."

"Is that all I am to you? A contract?"

The words came out almost curious, detached. Had she uttered those same words ten years ago, tears would already be pooling in her eyes, threatening to spill over as her voice trembled.

But that also meant he was going to have work harder to push her away, keep her from fighting this time.

"Yes."

She took a step forward. "I still don't believe you."

"Do you know why I was in Rome? Because your uncle asked me to check on you. It had nothing to do with you."

He'd expected the news to have more of an impact, but she just blinked.

"We only spent the past two weeks together because I agreed to do a loyal employee a favor and because we could help each other out." His jaw tightened. He needed to say it. Needed to push her away for the last time.

He'd expected tears. Insults. Something other than the long, long stare she gave him.

"You may not love me, but I think you felt something more than just casual lust for me," she finally said, her voice echoing over the pool and filling the space. "You're pushing me away like you did ten years ago. But," she added, holding up a hand as he started to speak, "you clearly don't trust me enough to share what happened. And for that reason, I'm ending our arrangement tonight."

The unexpected words locked him in place. "That's not what we agreed to."

"No." She raised her chin. "The situation has changed. I fell in love with you again."

Each syllable reverberated throughout his entire being. The last time she'd uttered those words, it had filled him with guilt and self-loathing. Plenty of both still existed, but after the happiness he'd found with her these past two weeks, it also filled him with a longing so strong he nearly gave in.

"I love you, Antonio," she repeated. "But you would rather stay in the past and keep your walls up than trust me. When you say you don't love me, I believe you, because if you did, I think you'd trust me enough to know I care about you, sins and all." Her head tilted to the side, some of the fire leaving her expression to be replaced by sadness. "Or, if what I think is true and you do care for me and you're just trying to do the noble thing, then you're repeating what you did back then and making a choice for me. Either way, hanging on to the past is more important to you than looking toward the future."

The air rushed out of his lungs as she reached

down, unhooked the bracelet and laid it on a small table next to one of the lounge chairs.

"You can keep it." His voice sounded strangled.

She shook her head. "No, thank you. Every time I would look at it, I'd think of why you bought it for me."

He frowned then closed his eyes as he remembered. He'd told her he'd bought the bracelet to play up their relationship for the cameras. Not because he'd wanted to, but because it looked good.

"I bought it for you, Anna."

Her smile this time was sad, fleeting. "We both know that's not true. But I appreciate it." She started to turn away.

His heart twisted, ordered him to stop her from leaving, but he managed to keep his feet rooted in place.

She paused. Glanced at him one last time with that blue-amber gaze. "I meant what I said that night at the restaurant. Thank you. For everything."

She turned.

In the blink of an eye, she was gone.

CHAPTER EIGHTEEN

ANNA WIPED ANOTHER pesky tear off her cheek as she propped her feet up on the metal railing of the balcony surrounding the rooftop. Someone had dragged an old metal chair up and left it there. She'd spent her first Sunday back, the morning she should have been at the wedding breakfast, painting it a yellow so bright it almost made her eyes hurt to look at in the direct sunlight.

But she'd needed something cheery. In the week since the wedding reception, she'd spent every morning and every evening on the roof, sipping a latte in the morning and a glass of wine at night as she evaluated her drawings of the day.

Thankfully, Sylvie Smythe had helped keep her mind off things. Her partnership with the legendary designer would be announced on Monday, followed by a whirlwind tour of Sylvie's existing European warehouses and then a trip across the sea to a new textile mill opening up next month just outside her old hometown.

Kess, who had dropped by to lend an ear and

brought a bottle of wine, had pronounced the opening of the mill as fate. She'd also denounced Antonio as the "biggest ass on the planet" and offered to set Anna up with a male model from Sweden that she promised would fulfill every one of Anna's dreams.

A sigh escaped her. She couldn't regret having Antonio as her first lover. Unfortunately, she suspected that every relationship she would have from here on out would be overshadowed by loving and losing him. Again.

Except this time, she'd been mature enough to see past the cruel words. Antonio had been hurting. He hadn't told her why, but she had made her own deductions. Seeing William, knowing he had been injured in a car accident the same week Antonio had ended their friendship. The way Antonio had tensed up in the car ride on the way down the mountain from the restaurant, how he never drove, his nightmarish mumblings in the night. His attempted rejection had bounced off her this time. No, what had hurt the most was that she had shared everything with him about her life, her fears, her insecurities, allowed him to pry into her hopes and dreams and talk her up.

Yet he hadn't trusted her enough to do the same.

Her hands curled around her mug of coffee, savoring the warmed ceramic. Fall had started to slip in early as August had turned to September. A cool wind blew through the streets, carrying the occasional leaf up over the rooftops. She stood and walked to the railing. The horn of a scooter filled the narrow alleyway and brought a sad smile to her face. That was the one thing they hadn't done in Positano: ride a scooter up and down the hilly streets. She'd asked, but Antonio had made excuses or whisked her away to something else every time.

She'd thought at first he hadn't wanted to look silly. She could hear his voice in her head, deep and with a faintly horrified tone. "A billionaire on a scooter?"

Now she knew better. Antonio didn't trust himself. Not to drive, not to love. Not to be happy. Amazing how much growing up and becoming stronger had done for her. Back then, the part that had hurt the most had been him not loving her back. What hurt now was knowing Antonio would probably keep himself in that hellish prison he'd created for himself for a very long time, possibly forever.

A buzzing drew her attention away from the rooftops of Paris. She padded back down the circular stairs and rushed to her front door where a frazzled-looking delivery woman stood, a box under her arm.

"Bonjour." The woman shoved a clipboard at her, showed her where to sign and then pushed the box into Anna's arms before disappearing back down the narrow hallway. Anna glanced at the

label and savored the little thrill that shot through her veins. The first true burst of happiness she'd felt since she'd woken up to an empty bed.

She brought the box inside and unwrapped it by the window. The standard cardboard shipping container contained a sturdier box, plain white with a small note on top in loopy cursive.

Congratulations on the upcoming line.

The wish from a shopkeeper she'd only met once made her smile. She closed her eyes, breathed in deeply, then opened them as she lifted the lid.

She had to rear back to keep tears from falling on the mounds of red silk inside. She reached inside, stroked the fabric. She'd accused Antonio of living in the past. Yet as she'd clicked through the photos of her and Antonio's time together, available online through a variety of media outlets, she'd seen images of herself touching the red silk that first full day in town. The silk she'd walked away from because she'd been unsure. After everything she'd accomplished, and still she'd hesitated.

No more.

Even if Antonio couldn't move forward, she would. For herself and in honor of the time they'd shared. And the possibility of what they could have been.

She reached into the box and pulled out the first bolt of fabric. She had some work to do.

Antonio stared down at the advanced copy of the November issue of the luxury fashion magazine. Had it really only been six weeks since he'd kicked her out of his life?

Anna had accomplished a lot in six weeks. Photos of her and Sylvie Smith had popped up everywhere. Despite his aversion to social media, he'd kept up with her daily posts on Instagram and what she was working on in her Paris flat. Usually, the camera was focused on her fabric, her sketches, her latest creation. But once in a while her hand appeared, or her feet crossed at the ankle as she sat on her rooftop holding up a square of fabric to the setting sun.

Ridiculous how much he savored those glimpses of her.

The media interest had initially flared when Sylvie Smythe had announced a partnership with up-and-coming designer Anna Vega. Each mention of Antonio had been met with a shy smile and a "No comment" from Anna and a snarky "Do you want to know about her work or not?" from Sylvie.

His brothers, mother and even his father had also been pestering him with texts and calls. But after the wedding breakfast, when he'd lied through his teeth that Anna had had to hurry back to Paris for an amazing opportunity, he'd disappeared to Positano to oversee the final phases before the grand opening Mornings were for reports. Afternoons for reviewing the work done that day.

And evenings...most evenings he spent holed up in his room, avoiding the balcony like the plague and sleeping on the couch. The couple of times he ventured into town, he avoided the places that reminded him of Anna. Hard to do when he saw her every time he passed someone eating lemon sorbet or sipping a glass of wine. Seeing couples zip by on scooters was the hardest. He knew she'd been crestfallen when he'd said no. It was absurd that even now he wouldn't get behind the wheel. How much damage could he do going ten miles an hour up and down teeny streets?

It hadn't been worth the risk to find out.

He was more than aware of the double standard he'd imposed, being so proud of Anna's journey to finding her own inner strength while he clung to the ruins of his own past. The nightmares kept him from picking up the phone, calling her or sending a quick text of congratulations, even if his heart fought him. They still plagued him, every night but now with a twist; no longer William's face but Anna's covered in blood and broken glass.

So different from the beautiful face gazing up at him. Anna's face, smiling at something off-camera as she sat on the floor of her flat surrounded by silk. *Her* silk, he'd realized when he'd seen the magazine on a stand outside a little shop in town and bought it before he'd been able to talk himself out of it. The title declared Anna Vega: Rising Star of Sustainable Fashion. The diamond bracelet had sparkled from where it sat on the corner of his desk, cold and hard. The opposite of Anna. He'd seen her looking at the silk, had thought of purchasing it for her. But it had unnerved him, the thought of doing something so personal, so he'd bought the most impersonal thing he could find.

...hanging on to the past is more important to you than looking toward the future.

His hands tightened on the magazine. Perhaps he would go down to the gym this evening, run on the treadmill until his body was so exhausted he couldn't think of blue-amber eyes and a smile that made him warm and possessive. His fingers settled on the pages. Did he dare open it? Further torture himself by reading her words, seeing more photos?

His phone buzzed. He glanced at the number and answered.

"Yes, Paul?"

"Sir, your guests are here."

"My what? Paul, we don't open for another two weeks."

"That's what I told them, sir, but—"

"*¡Mi hermano!* Call off your guard dog and get your stupid *culo* down here."

The muscles in his neck tightened as Alejandro's voice rang out.

"What are you doing here?"

A scuffling sound ensued, followed by an even deeper voice. "We're here to knock some sense into you."

Adrian. He leaned back in his chair and tossed the magazine onto his desk. It was only a matter of time before his older brothers came knocking.

"I don't know if I have any rooms available."

"Of course you do."

Antonio rolled his eyes. Adrian always had been a self-assured bastard. He'd assumed some of his brother's mannerisms; aloofness, professionalism, an air of confidence that made most people believe what he said. But now that he heard it tossed back at him, he had to wonder if he sounded that pompous.

"You wouldn't turn away your pregnant sisters-in-law, would you?"

His eyes fluttered shut. Dear God, had they brought the whole damned family?

"Antonio?"

His eyes flew open at the sound of Isabella's voice. Apparently, they had.

"Please may we come up?"

With a long-suffering sigh, he told Paul to bring them up. Minutes later, his brothers and mother crowded into his office. The room that had felt so large when he'd claimed it as his own shrunk as Adrian stalked to his desk, Alejandro tossed himself into one of the leather chairs, and Isabella walked around the room, her maternal curiosity making her stop and examine everything from the books on his shelves to the framed pictures.

"Where are Calandra and Everleigh?"

"Downstairs with Father," Alejandro said.

"Father's here, too?"

Could this day get any worse?

"What happened between you and Anna?" Adrian demanded, placing his hands on the desk and leaning forward. A power move meant to intimidate. But Antonio had learned from the best. He leaned back in his chair, his fingers forming a steeple as he met Adrian's dark stare.

"None of your concern."

"It is when my little brother is ruining his life. Again."

Anger surged through him and propelled him to his feet.

"Careful, *hermano*." His voice turned to ice, even as his gaze flitted to Isabella. He didn't want her knowing his shameful secret. He was the only man in this family who hadn't caused her pain. To do so now, after so many years and when she was going through her own hell with her husband…

"I know."

He froze then looked away. He couldn't look

at her. Couldn't bear to see the disappointment, the hurt.

The rejection.

"How could you?" he managed to grit out. He had never once hit his brothers. But now his fingers itched to do just that.

"I didn't." Adrian nodded toward the door. "He did."

Antonio's head swung around, his pulse pounding so loud he couldn't believe it didn't echo off the walls of his office. A room that suddenly felt like a prison as William Tomàs appeared in the doorway.

The details he'd glimpsed at the wedding—the cane, the scar, the slight drag to his right foot— all sharpened with less than twenty feet between them. When William smiled, the scar stretched into a gruesome curve.

"Hello, Tony."

Say something.

"William."

William walked into the room. Shuffled, was more like it, each step intentional, the click of the cane on the hardwood floor deafening and damning.

"It's been a long time."

"Sí."

William drew closer, his eyes searching Antonio's face.

"You stupid bastard."

After the letter William had written him, the edges now worn, the ink faded from being unfolded, read and refolded so many times, he hadn't expected to hear such words from his former friend. "What?"

"Did you even read the letter I wrote you back?"

Antonio frowned, aware that four pairs of eyes were watching him intently.

"Yes. Doesn't change that I caused the car accident that left you disabled, William. You didn't want to go that night, and I pushed you." His hand jabbed toward the cane. "If I hadn't pushed you, you wouldn't need that thing."

William frowned. "I didn't want to go because I had just broken up with Abigail and was wallowing in self-pity. But I agreed, didn't I? And as I recall, I was egging you on, telling you to go faster."

A dim echo sounded in his head. William's voice. *Seriously? I came out for you to drive like an* abuela? *Punch it!*

William walked around the desk and put his hand on Antonio's shoulder. If he saw Antonio flinch, he didn't mention it.

"I've moved on, Tony." A grin split his face. "I'm in my final year of medical school in America. The accident set me on a path I'd never even thought of. This time next year, I'll be completing my residency in pediatrics."

Antonio swallowed hard. "I didn't know."

"I figured after you didn't respond to my last

letter that you didn't have an interest in being friends anymore." The grin disappeared as William's jaw tightened. "I had no idea it was because you were still carrying so much guilt. And if that's the reason you're no longer with Anna, then you're a damned fool."

A muscle ticced in Antonio's cheek. "The doctor told me you didn't remember what happened. But I do. I relive it over and over again. The pain I caused you, the time I stole from you. Do you know why I asked you to go with me that night?" he bit out. Suddenly, he didn't care. Let them know everything. Then they could all know what he'd known all along; that he was unworthy. "Because I was falling for Anna. My best friend, seventeen years old, still in school, and I wanted to go do something wild so I could stop thinking about her."

The words hung in the air, so silent, he could hear the varied breathing of everyone staring at him.

Alejandro broke the silence.

"Good God, man, that's why?"

"Yes," Antonio snapped. "Even if I didn't deserve to be happy after what I did, I'm too selfish for someone like Anna. She deserves the best. That's not me. Never will be."

"Antonio, there was only two years difference between you two," Adrian pointed out matter-offactly. "Had you dated her the year before, you would have both still been in school."

When phrased like that, his attraction suddenly didn't seem nearly so illicit. Yet he'd felt so much older that summer, more worldly after his year away.

"Have you seen how I used to deal with bad situations?" Alejandro broke in.

"Chandelier in Vegas," Adrian muttered.

"Everyone brings that up." Alejandro's grin said he didn't mind. "Going fast on a mountain road is nothing." A grimace crossed his face. "I can't count the number of times I could have seriously hurt someone with the way I used to behave. You just had bad luck to have the first time you tried to rebel result in something dire."

"But I didn't do things like that, period. I was the good son."

"Oh, Antonio." Isabella's eyes welled with tears. "You are a good son, but that doesn't mean you had to be perfect."

His throat closed. "I never wanted to hurt you. I wanted to make you happy."

"And you do!" Isabella moved forward and cupped his face in his hands. "How did I not notice that you took on such responsibility? My happiness was my own to manage. That I refused to see the problems your father and I had, or not communicate with your brothers, was my burden to bear, not yours."

"Nor was it your responsibility to try to fill the gaps Alejandro and I left," Adrian said. A slight smile crossed his face. "Remember how you told me years ago you hated being in debt to us for helping you and William that night? I've just realized that he and I are in your debt for seeing what we couldn't and trying to fix the pain we caused our family."

"Plus," Alejandro added, "if you think you're too selfish for Anna, I'd say trying to be the perfect son for years to make our mother happy nixes that thought. Which means you need to call her, grovel, and hope she'll take you back."

As the words of his loved ones sank in, the ties that had kept him bound loosened, fell away. A lightness crept in, regret and shock and relief swirling together in a heady combination.

William wrapped an arm around Antonio's shoulders and pulled him into a bear hug. "Go be happy. You deserve it."

Antonio clapped him on the back, his throat constricting. When he stood back, it was to see William grinning from ear to ear. The scar no longer stood out. Just the glimpse of the boy Antonio had once known and the man he'd become.

Isabella moved to his side and enfolded him in an embrace. "My child." She leaned back and smiled. "Despite your ridiculous height, always my child. Not my husband, not my protector. It was not your job to assume so much responsibility, and I'm so sorry I didn't see it sooner."

"I'm sorry, too," Adrian chimed in. "*Madre* and I...we had a lot to work through. Still do." He came up and put an arm around her shoulders, pressing a kiss to her forehead that put another sparkling sheen of tears in her eyes. "But it's much better now."

"Father and I are even getting along," Alejandro added from the chair. "Telling him we're having his first grandchild helped matters."

Adrian rolled his eyes. "By a month."

"What about Father?" Antonio asked, his gaze going back to his mother. "At the wedding, you said things weren't going well."

"They weren't." Isabella sighed. "I was in a bad place for a long time. I maintained a rosy view of what your father and I had. I made excuses for him not being there, for him not being involved in your lives. He shared some things with me this summer, too, that hurt very deeply." She inhaled, her shoulders straightening. "But he's working on himself, just as I'm working on myself. We want to make our marriage work. It's not easy. It's very, very hard. But sometimes you have to fight harder than others."

Antonio let out a harsh breath. "Anna and I... relationship wasn't what you think it was."

"Drop the pretense, baby brother." Alejandro stood in one fluid motion and stalked closer. "Adrian overheard you fighting at the reception."

"What exactly did you hear?" Antonio asked with a glance at Adrian.

"Every word. The fake relationship was a nice touch. Although," Adrian added, "it looked damn real to me in those photos."

It had felt real, too.

"She won't want to be with me. Not after I pushed her away."

Isabella shook her head. "I can't believe that. Not with the way she looked at you."

"You don't understand, *Madre*. I've hurt her so much."

"That's a risk we all take when we care about someone."

All heads swung toward Alejandro.

"What?" He grinned. "I'm in love. And so are you, even if you deny it," he added to Antonio.

Adrian hit something on the screen of his phone then handed it to Antonio. His heart twisted. It was a tabloid article, the headline screaming Hotel Billionaire and Childhood Sweetheart Indulge in Ice Cream in Italy.

Sorbet, he mentally ground out. But then his eyes landed on the picture. Anna's eyes were partially shut, her mouth open in a laugh as sorbet dripped over her fingers. A photo most women would shudder to see; normalcy instead of poised elegance.

But Anna looked happy. Happy and beautiful and joyful, her dark hair pulled up into a ponytail, her mint-colored skirt and white blouse shown off to perfection against her tanned skin.

His gaze slid over. In the photo, he was smiling at Anna. Truly smiling, his lips curved up at the corners, his eyes crinkled as he watched her. It had been early in the second week, after he'd taken her to bed. One hand rested on her knee, fingers splayed across her skin that he remembered had felt like warm silk beneath his touch. She made him enjoy the little things in life, achieve a balance that had eluded him until she'd literally landed back in his life and offered him her heart once more.

"*Dios mío*, what have I done?"

"Get him the whiskey," Adrian ordered.

Alejandro pressed a glass into Antonio's hands.

"Don't worry. Alejandro and I have both been where you're at."

"Just a couple months' ago, actually," Alejandro added cheerfully. "And look at us now."

"I said things to her...horrible things." The whiskey burned a trail down his throat, but also banished some of the panic threatening to burst in.

"Yeah, I think you said even worse things than Adrian did when he broke things off with Everleigh."

"Not helping, Alejandro," Adrian ground out.

"None of you are helping!" Isabella clapped her

hands. "Adrian and Alejandro, go to your wives. William, darling, Paul will set you up with your room. Once my youngest has gotten Anna to forgive him, I'm sure he'll want to catch up with you."

Twenty seconds later the room was cleared, the door closed. Antonio sank into the chair Alejandro had recently vacated, pressure building behind his forehead.

What have I done? What have I done? What have I done?

"Tony." He looked up to see his mother's compassionate face in front of him. "She loves you."

"Love isn't always enough."

"No. But it can be a start." She kissed his forehead before leaving him alone to his thoughts.

He needed to tell Anna how he truly felt, that much was obvious. But just telling her wouldn't be enough. No, he needed to prove that he was moving beyond the past. Setting his sights on the future and moving on.

A thought popped into his head. He'd failed miserably with the diamond bracelet. She'd already bought the silk. But there was another gift he could give her, something she truly wanted that would also show her he could move on.

He tossed back the rest of the whiskey, set the glass down and stood. Anna had been so brave, telling him how she'd felt all those years ago and then again at the wedding. She had no idea how incredible she was, how resilient and courageous.

Now it was his time to be strong for her. And, God willing, she still loved him.

CHAPTER NINETEEN

ANNA GLANCED DOWN at her phone again and frowned. Kess had said she would pick her up at four p.m. A chill had settled across Rome, the cold sinking into the stones and chasing tourists off the street as the sun started to set.

Fortunately, when Sylvie Smythe's fashion show at the Trevi Fountain took place in three days, the temperature would be more agreeable, a little warm for early November. But then again, Anna thought with a smile, Sylvie had probably ordered it that way.

It had all moved so fast. The magazine feature, written by a new writer. Sylvie had suggested the publisher drop Leo White. Last Anna heard, he was writing for some conspiracy theory tabloid in the US. Her designs had come together in record time. In three days, they would be featured on a see-through runway that would run across the bubbling water of the world's most famous fountain.

The first time Anna had laid eyes on the fountain two days ago, she'd barely bit back a sob. It had been over two months since she'd last seen Antonio. There had been no calls, no text messages, no emails. He'd said it was over, and he'd truly meant it.

She still didn't regret it. None of it. But, dear God, it hurt so much more than she could have ever prepared herself for.

Thank goodness for Sylvie and Kess. At Anna's suggestion, Sylvie had snatched up her friend as producer for the show. Not only had Kess put together a dynamite show, but she had managed to sneak a couple of hours away for an early dinner.

Anna glanced down. Kess had said they were going somewhere nice, and had suggested Anna wear one of her red-silk creations. She hadn't worn any of them. It had been too painful. But Kess had practically begged, pointing out that she would most likely be photographed while they were out and about, and pictures of her work would only help bolster the show.

So she'd pulled out this dress, a vintage-inspired creation with a full skirt, a square neckline and sleeves down to her elbows. Classy and sophisticated, topped off with a white pea coat and matching gloves.

A tiny beep-beep sounded. A scooter. She looked up, a smile starting to form. Before she left Rome, she would most definitely be renting one to see the sights.

A bright blue scooter rounded the corner. It took a moment for her eyes to drift up, to see the person at the helm.

When she did, her heart stopped.

Antonio.

He stopped the scooter in front of her, the tire skidding a little on the street. He winced then turned to her with a grin that restarted her heart and kicked it into overdrive.

"A little harder to drive these things than I thought." His eyes latched onto hers, burning with intensity. "I missed you, Anna."

Had he truly said those words out loud? She'd longed to hear them, had dreamed of him whispering that and other sweet phrases at night, only to wake up over and over to the realization that he was no longer a part of her life.

Except now he was here. In Rome. Again.

She swallowed hard, a million questions running through her mind. *Why?* was a popular one, followed by *How did you find me?* What popped out was, "I can't believe you fit on one of those things." If he didn't look so damned handsome, it would almost be comical.

He smiled a little then inhaled deeply and extended a hand. "I know I've done absolutely nothing to earn your trust. But I'd like to take you on a ride and explain."

"I'm waiting on Kess."

"Actually, you're not." He had the good grace to

look slightly abashed. "I roped her into my plan. She's working tonight."

Anna looked skyward. Her friend meant well. But right now she'd love nothing more than to strangle Kess and her romantic tendencies.

"Ten minutes, Anna. Ten minutes and, if at the end, you never want to see me again, I promise to never contact you."

She'd found herself at so many crossroads lately. Making decisions and taking risks had proved to be mostly beneficial, but sometimes it was utterly exhausting. Part of her wanted to turn around, go back up to her hotel room, crawl beneath the covers and cry.

But if she didn't take this risk, she knew a part of her would always wonder.

Her fingers settled in his. Her breath hissed out between her teeth at the electricity that arced between them. He brought her hand up to his lips and pressed a kiss to her knuckles that made warmth pool between her thighs.

Perhaps this is a bad idea.

Before she could ruminate on that, he tugged her forward. She swung a leg over and sat on the little seat behind him. He handed her a helmet. As soon as she had it buckled on, he reached back for her hand once more.

"Put your arms around me."

Did he have to sound so seductive? She leaned forward, her arms slowly wrapping around his waist, doing her best to ignore how good his body felt, how familiar and comforting his scent was.

And then they were off, cruising along the streets of Rome, cafés and shops flashing past as light spilled forth from their windows.

"The first time you told me you loved me," he said over his shoulder, his voice slightly raised so he could be heard, "it was three days after I got into a car accident."

Her arms tightened around him. She'd suspected as much, but to hear it spoken out loud made her heart ache for him. More questions arose, but she bit them back.

"William Tomàs was in the car. He was hurt very badly." Guilt and grief made his voice heavy and tightened the muscles in his back. She wanted to rub her hands over him, soothe the pain away as her heart broke for the young man who had nearly lost a friend. "We were up on the mountain, going to a party. I was driving too fast, lost control of the wheel and wrapped the car around the tree. I wasn't hurt, but William was. By some terrible twist of fate, the ambulances were all engaged for a big wreck in Granada and wouldn't have made it in time. I called Adrian, who by some miracle was at home. He and Alejandro drove up, took William and me to the hospital." His voice dropped so low, she could barely hear his next words as he turned onto a little side street. "You saw the cane. That's because of me."

Tears pooled in her eyes. "I'm sorry."

He kept one hand on the handlebars of the scooter, but another came down to rest on her hands clasped around his waist. A gentle squeeze and then he resumed.

"I was torn up about you. After the picnic, I wanted you. Physically. It's why I went to the party, to distract myself because I didn't know what to do. I was nineteen. I didn't think I wanted to get married or have kids. But I knew you did and, to enter into a relationship with my friend who did want those things when all I could think about was sex, seemed so cruel. And after William's accident, I felt...toxic. I'd always been the good one, doing the right thing. The one time I deviated from being the good son, and I nearly got my best friend killed."

She started to say something, to reassure him. He must have sensed it, because he glanced over his shoulder and held up a hand. "It's hard for me to talk about this. I need to get it all out, and then I'll listen to whatever you have to say."

She nodded. She had no idea where this conversation was going, how it would end. So she gave in to temptation and let her head drop against his back, her cheek rubbing against the cozy warmth of his blazer.

"After the accident, the physical desire I felt for you seemed even more wrong. Crude. You were so beautiful and pure and innocent, and I felt like a murderer."

The tears spilled forth and dampened the back of his coat. Her heart ached. Why hadn't he just told her? Even if he hadn't returned her romantic feelings, she would have been there for him. As a friend. Had he truly not trusted her?

As if he could read her mind, he said, "I withdrew from everyone after that. My mother, my brothers. I felt so guilty for what happened to William, humiliated that I had prided myself on being the good son only to go and do something so stupid that rivaled anything Adrian or Alejandro had done. And I started to live my life very rigidly after that. I never drove. No play. No fun. No exceptions."

The scooter slowed. She lifted her head just as the Trevi Fountain came into view. Antonio parked the scooter next to a building, helped her off and set their helmets on the back of the scooter. Even with the barrier of her gloves, the warmth from his hand seeped through. She followed as he tugged her toward the fountain, the surrounding plaza mostly deserted. The ramifications of what he'd done, operating a vehicle for the first time in ten years, hit her and fanned the flames of her hope.

"And then you landed in my lap, Anna." His hand came up, faltered, then slowly settled on her cheek, cupping her face with an exquisite tenderness. "Still joyful, innocent. And yet so strong. The desire was still there. The friendship was still there. But something new was, too."

Her breath hitched at the emotion brimming in his mahogany eyes. She wanted to believe it, wanted so badly to think it was possible, but did she dare?

"Love, Anna." He leaned down, pausing to see if she would turn away. When she didn't, he pressed his forehead to hers, his breath coming out in a rush. "I fell in love with you. I fell in love and I was so consumed with the past, with seeing myself as unworthy of love and too selfish to deserve someone like you."

Her eyes drifted shut, tears clinging to her lashes. "I thought you didn't love me."

"Open your eyes."

She did, her lips trembling at what she saw on his face.

"I love you, Anna. So much. And I will spend the rest of my life making it up to you. If you'll let me."

Her mouth dropped open. "What?"

He reached into his pocket. Her heart started to beat faster. His fingers uncurled to reveal...

Three cents?

She stared at the coins in confusion. Coins?

Then the rhyme returned. Her head snapped up, hope tearing through her so quickly it nearly made her dizzy.

Three coins and you'll be married soon.

"Antonio…"

"I have prayed every night for the last two weeks that you still feel about me the way you did the night of Alejandro's wedding. Because if you do…" His other hand disappeared into his pocket and came out with a black-velvet box. "I hope this diamond will be one you'll wear knowing it is solely because I love you."

Had she thought she'd taken risks before? Because none of the risks she'd taken in the last ten months meant anything compared to what lay before her now. Antonio had hurt her not once but twice in spectacular fashion. Could she trust him again?

"I know I hurt you," he whispered, reading her mind once more. "I know loving me after what I've put you through is a risk. I can't promise I won't hurt you again, because love is not perfect. But I can promise I will spend the rest of my life doing whatever I can to make you as happy as you deserve to be, and striving to be the best man I can be." He swallowed hard. "You make me feel like the best version of myself, Anna. I can't picture my life without you and I want you to be mine, forever and always."

It was the most realistic declaration of love she'd ever heard, one that paled in comparison to any love story she'd watched or read. With a tremulous smile, she reached down and scooped the three coins out of his hand. She turned her back, tossed them over her shoulder and listened as they fell into the fountain. When she turned back to Antonio, it was to see a mix of love and desire and hope in his eyes.

"Is that a yes?"

She flung her arms around his neck, threw back her head and laughed as he scooped her up in his arms and swung her around in a circle.

Somewhere off to their right, a light flashed.

"Damned paparazzi," Antonio swore. "I'll kill—"

Anna cupped his face in her hands and kissed him, cutting off his remaining statement.

"Think of it this way," she said as she pulled back. "We'll always have a picture of your proposal."

His laugh rang out across the plaza. "Are you always so positive?"

"Better get used to it." Her face hurt from smiling so hard as he set her down and slid the diamond ring onto her finger, the oval-cut beauty offset by two gems, a blue sapphire and an amber-colored topaz. "Because I'm positively in love with you."

EPILOGUE

Three years later

ANTONIO CHASED HIS niece Ava through the waves, the two-year-old's squeal making him grin. Just a few steps ahead of her, his nephew Xavier scrambled up onto the warm sand.

"Xavier, why don't you give Tío Tony a break?" Calandra called. She was relaxing on one of the chaises-longue, her six-months-pregnant belly round and evident even in her black swimsuit.

"I don't mind," Antonio called up. Besides, he needed the practice. He glanced over at his wife as she chatted with Everleigh and Everleigh's father. His gaze drifted down to her stomach, concealed by the loose fabric of her sundress. Excitement zipped through him. They planned to make their announcement this evening at dinner when the whole family was gathered. Not just the Cabreras, but Calandra's little sister and her boyfriend from North Carolina, and Richard Bradford and his former housekeeper now girlfriend. William had joined them, too, along with Kess.

Although, Antonio reflected with a smile, those two hadn't been seen since dinner last night. He'd had his suspicions with the verbal sparring they had engaged in since they'd arrived for the annual family summer trip to Positano last week. Perhaps the family would be celebrating another wedding soon.

Adrian dashed into the waves and scooped Ava up into his arms. The little girl let out a squeal of delight before turning and wrapping her chubby arms around her father's neck.

"When are you going to have one of these?" Adrian asked with a boyish grin.

"Someday soon," Anna answered with a conspiratorial grin aimed Antonio's way as she walked into the warm waters of Le Porto's private beach. Antonio had set aside three hours for the family to enjoy the cove before reopening it to the guests of the hotel. Given that the hotel had become Positano's number-one choice for luxury vacations and had received award after award since its grand opening, he'd felt confident notifying his guests that the beach would be briefly closed for a private gathering.

Antonio pulled his wife close and kissed her.

"Eww!" Xavier squealed before dashing up the beach to his grandparents. Javier scooted over on his lounge and hauled the little boy up onto his lap.

It still took some getting used to, seeing his formerly buttoned-up sire act like a teenager around his grandchildren. But Javier Cabrera had undergone a truly remarkable transformation, building relationships not just with his grandchildren but his sons as well.

"I want to tell them now," Antonio said, his hand sliding down to cup her belly. He knew it was too soon, but already he imagined her stomach round, the feeling of new life kicking beneath his fingers.

"No!" Anna said with a laugh as she batted his hand away. "Tonight."

"Did you hear from Sylvie?"

Anna nodded, her smile rivaling that of the sun shining overhead. "Another record-breaking quarter."

Antonio kissed her cheek. Anna insisted that the cult following her designs had developed was possible because of Sylvie. But in the conversations he'd had with the older woman, he knew that Anna had revitalized the legendary designer's brand. Her stunning designs, her passion for sustainable clothing and her genuine kindness had drawn in and retained thousands of new shoppers.

"Do you remember when you were first here and didn't know if you'd make it as a designer?"

Anna rolled her eyes. "Blah-blah-blah. Yes, for the hundredth time, you were right."

He tugged her closer, savoring the feel of her in his arms. "I was right about something else, too."

She looked up at him, smiled. "Oh, yeah?"

"Yeah. You're mine. Forever and always."

* * * * *

Enchanted by
A Deal for the Tycoon's Diamonds?
Check out the first and second instalments in
The Infamous Cabrera Brothers trilogy:

His Billion-Dollar Takeover Temptation
Proof of Their One Hot Night

And be sure to check out
Emmy Grayson's next story, coming soon!